CHANDA'S SECRETS

ALLAN STRATTON

annick press
toronto+new york+vancouver

© 2004 by Allan Stratton

Fourteenth printing, November 2013

Annick Press Ltd.

All rights reserved. No part of this work covered by the copyrights hereon may be reproduced or used in any form or by any means—graphic, electronic, or mechanical—without the prior written permission of the publisher.

We acknowledge the support of the Canada Council for the Arts, the Ontario Arts Council, and the Government of Canada through the Canada Book Fund (CBF) for our publishing activities.

The publisher acknowledges with thanks the Canadian International Development Agency and the Federation of Canadian Municipalities for their support in the development of this publication.

Editing by Barbara Pulling
Copy editing by Elizabeth McLean
Interior design by Irvin Cheung/iCheung Design
Cover design by Monica Charny and Irvin Cheung/iCheung Design
Cover image used with permission of Bavaria Film International/Bavaria Media GmbH
Line drawings by Warren Clark
The text was typeset in Sabon

Cataloging in Publication

Stratton, Allan

    Chanda's secrets / by Allan Stratton.

ISBN 978-1-55037-835-1 (bound).—ISBN 978-1-55037-834-4 (pbk.)

    I. Title.

PS8587.T723C45 2004   C813'.54   C2003-906069-1

Published in the U.S.A. by	**Distributed in Canada by**	**Distributed in the U.S.A. by**
Annick Press (U.S.) Ltd.	Firefly Books Ltd.	Firefly Books (U.S.) Inc.
	50 Staples Ave., Unit 1	P.O. Box 1338
	Richmond Hill, ON	Ellicott Station
	L4B 0A7	Buffalo, NY 14205

Printed and bound in Canada.

MIX
Paper from
responsible sources
FSC
www.fsc.org **FSC® C004071**

Visit our website at: www.annickpress.com
Also available in e-book format. Please visit
www.annickpress.com/ebooks.html
for more details. Or scan

Visit Allan Stratton's website at: www.allanstratton.com

A Teacher's Guide is available that offers a program of classroom study based on this book. It is available free at www.annickpress.com

THANKS

I owe so much to so many people in Botswana, Zimbabwe, South Africa, and Kenya; without their friendship, guidance, and support, this book could never have been written. In particular, I want to thank Patricia Bakwinya, Tebogoc Bakwinya, and Chanda Selalame of the Tshireletso AIDS Awareness Group; Solomon Kamwendo and his theater company Ghetto Artists; Rogers Bande and Anneke Viser of COCEPWA (Coping Centre for People Living with HIV/AIDS); Angelina Magaga of The Light and Courage Centre; Professor K. Osei-Hwedie of the University of Botswana; the young people of PACT (Peer Approach to Counseling by Teens); Banyana Parsons of The Kagisano Women's Shelter Project; Richard and John Cox; and the many individuals and families who invited me into their homes, whether in town, village, or cattle post. From Canada, I'd like to thank the Ontario Arts Council and the Toronto Arts Council; Barbara Emanuel; Mary Coyle and Kim MacPherson of the Coady International Institute; and all the folks at Annick Press, especially my editor, Barbara Pulling, and my copy editor, Elizabeth McLean.

For those who are passed and those who survive

AUTHOR'S NOTE

Sub-Saharan Africa comprises a number of independent nations, each with its own political, social, and cultural histories. *Chanda's Secrets* is a personal story about one young woman and her family. They live in a fictional country, which is not intended to represent the unique complexities of any existing country, nor to encompass the wide range of differences, histories, and experiences to be found within the sub-Saharan region. The characters are likewise fictional.

I

I'M ALONE IN THE OFFICE of Bateman's Eternal Light Funeral Services. It's early Monday morning and Mr. Bateman is busy with a new shipment of coffins.

"I'll get to you as soon as I can," he told me. "Meanwhile, you can go into my office and look at my fish. They're in an aquarium on the far wall. If you get bored, there're magazines on the coffee table. By the way, I'm sorry about your sister."

I don't want to look at Mr. Bateman's fish. And I certainly don't want to read. I just want to get this meeting over with before I cry and make a fool of myself.

Mr. Bateman's office is huge. It's also dark. The blinds are closed and half the fluorescent lights are burned out. Aside from the lamp on his desk, most of the light in the room comes from the aquarium. That's fine, I guess. The darkness hides the junk piled in the corners: hammers, boards, paint cans, saws, boxes of nails, and a stepladder. Mr. Bateman renovated the place six months ago, but he hasn't tidied up yet.

Before the renovations, Bateman's Eternal Light didn't do funerals. It was a building supply center. That's why it's located between a lumber yard and a place that rents cement mixers. Mr. Bateman opened it when he arrived from England eight years ago. It was always busy, but these days, despite the building boom, there's more money in death than construction.

The day of the grand reopening, Mr. Bateman announced plans to have a chain of Eternal Lights across the country within two years. When reporters asked if he had any training in embalming, he said no, but he was completing a correspondence course from some college in the States. He also promised to hire the best hair stylists in town, and to offer discount rates. "No matter how poor, there's a place for everyone at Bateman's."

That's why I'm here.

When Mr. Bateman finally comes in, I don't notice. Somehow I've ended up on a folding chair in front of his aquarium staring at an angelfish. It's staring back. I wonder what it's thinking. I wonder if it knows it's trapped in a tank for the rest of its life. Or maybe it's happy swimming back and forth between the plastic grasses, nibbling algae from the turquoise pebbles and investigating the little pirate chest with the lid that blows air bubbles. I've loved angelfish ever since I saw pictures of them in a collection of *National Geographics* some missionaries donated to my school.

"So sorry to have kept you," Mr. Bateman says.

I leap to my feet.

"Sit, sit. Please," he smiles.

We shake hands and I sink back into the folding chair. He sits opposite me in an old leather recliner. There's a tear on the armrest with gray stuffing poking out. Mr. Bateman picks at it.

"Are we expecting your papa?"

"No," I say. "My step-papa's working." That's a lie. My step-papa is dead drunk at the neighborhood shebeen.

"Are we waiting for your mama, then?"

"She can't come either. She's very sick." This part is almost true. Mama is curled up on the floor, rocking my sister. When I told her we had to find a mortuary she just kept rocking. "You go," she whispered. "You're sixteen. I know you'll do what needs doing. I have to stay with my Sara."

Mr. Bateman clears his throat. "Might there be an auntie coming, then? Or an uncle?"

"No."

"Ah." His mouth bobs open and shut. His skin is pale and scaly. He reminds me of one of his fish. "Ah," he says again. "So you've been sent to make the arrangements by yourself."

I nod and stare at the small cigarette burn on his lapel. "I'm sixteen."

"Ah." He pauses. "How old was your sister?"

"Sara's one and a half," I say. "Was one and a half."

"One and a half. My, my." Mr. Bateman clucks his tongue. "It's always a shock when they're infants."

A shock? Sara was alive two hours ago. She was cranky all night because of her rash. Mama rocked her through dawn, till she stopped whining. At first we thought she'd just fallen asleep. (God, please forgive me for being angry with her last night. I didn't mean what I prayed. Please let this not be my fault.)

I lower my eyes.

Mr. Bateman breaks the silence. "You'll be glad you chose Eternal Light," he confides. "It's more than a mortuary. We provide embalming, a hearse, two wreaths, a small chapel, funeral programs and a mention in the local paper."

I guess this is supposed to make me feel better. It doesn't. "How much will it cost?" I ask.

"That depends," Mr. Bateman says. "What sort of funeral would you like?"

My hands flop on my lap. "Something simple, I guess."

"A good choice."

I nod. It's obvious I can't pay much. I got my dress from a ragpicker at the bazaar, and I'm dusty and sweaty from my bicycle ride here.

"Would you like to start by selecting a coffin?" he asks.

"Yes, please."

Mr. Bateman leads me to his showroom. The most expensive coffins are up front, but he doesn't want to insult me by whisking me to the back. Instead I get the full tour. "We stock a full line of products," he says. "Models come in pine and mahogany, and can be fitted with a variety of brass handles and bars. We have beveled edges, or plain. As for the linings, we offer silk, satin, and polyester in a range of colors. Plain pillowcases for the head rest are standard, but we can sew on a lace ribbon for free."

The more Mr. Bateman talks, the more excited he gets, giving each model a little rub with his handkerchief. He explains the difference between coffins and caskets: "Coffins have flat lids. Caskets have round lids." Not that it makes a difference. In the end, they're all boxes.

I'm a little frightened. We're getting to the back of the showroom and the price tags on the coffins are still an average year's wages. My step-papa does odd jobs, my mama keeps a few chickens and a vegetable garden, my sister is five and a half, my brother is four, and I'm in high school. Where is the money going to come from?

Mr. Bateman sees the look on my face. "For children's funerals, we have a less costly alternative," he says. He leads me behind a curtain into a back room and flicks on a light bulb. All around me, stacked to the ceiling, are tiny whitewashed coffins, dusted with yellow, pink, and blue spray paint.

Mr. Bateman opens one up. It's made of pressboards, held together with a handful of finishing nails. The lining is a plastic sheet, stapled in place. Tin handles are glued to the outside; if you tried to use them, they'd fall off.

I look away.

Mr. Bateman tries to comfort. "We wrap the children in a beautiful white shroud. Then we fluff the material over the sides of the box. All you see is the little face. Sara will look lovely."

I'm numb as he takes me back to the morgue, where she'll be kept till she's ready. He points at a row of oversized filing cabinets. "They're clean as a whistle, and fully refrigerated," he assures me. "Sara will have her own compartment, unless other children are brought in, of course, in which case she'll have to share."

We return to the office and Mr. Bateman hands me a contract. "If you've got the money handy, I'll drive by for the body at one. Sara will be ready for pickup Wednesday afternoon. I'll schedule the burial for Thursday morning."

I swallow hard. "Mama would like to hold off until the weekend. Our relatives need time to come in from the country."

"I'm afraid there's no discount on weekends," Mr. Bateman says, lighting a cigarette.

"Then maybe next Monday, a week today?"

"Not possible. I'll be up to my ears in new customers. I'm sorry. There're so many deaths these days. It's not me. It's the market."

2

I SIGN THE CONTRACT AND RUN OUTSIDE. Biking into the morning rush hour, I recite the alphabet over and over to make my mind go blank. It doesn't. I keep seeing that coffin with its pink pressboards, staples, and plastic sheet.

"Esther!" I think. "I have to see Esther!" Esther's my best friend. She'll give me a hug and tell me everything will be all right.

I veer left on the off chance she's at the nearby Liberty Hotel and Convention Center. Since her parents died, Esther's hardly ever in school. When she's not working for her auntie and uncle, which is mostly, she's posing for tourists in front of the hotel's Statue of Liberty fountain.

By the time I pull up, the circular drive is already plugged with buses, limos, and taxis. Bellhops are hauling the luggage of tour groups en route to safari. Chauffeurs are opening doors for foreign businessmen here to see the diamond mines. UN aid workers are catching rides for government buildings. But there's no Esther.

"Maybe they shooed her away," I think. When Esther gets the boot, she goes down the road to the Red Fishtail Mall. Usually she hangs around Mr. Mpho's Electronics, watching the wall of TVs in the window or listening to the music pumped over the outdoor speakers. After about twenty minutes, the Liberty's security guards are off doing something else and she drifts back.

I zip past a row of new offices and casinos, and into the mall parking lot, dodging cars and shopping carts as I ride by fancy stores selling kitchen and bathroom appliances. It must be nice to have electricity, not to mention running water.

Today there's no one in front of Mr. Mpho's except Simon, the beggar man with no legs; he has a bowl in front of him, a battered skateboard at his side. His eyes are half closed. He taps the back of his head against the cement window ledge in time to the music.

I peek inside the Internet cafe next door. Last week I saw Esther at a keyboard. I thought I was hallucinating. There she was in her bright orange flip-flops and her secondhand sequined halter top, popping gum and clicking the mouse.

"What are you doing here?" I asked.

"Getting my e-mails," she replied smugly.

I laughed in her face. There's a computer in the main office at school, and we've all been taken down to see how it works, but the idea of using one in real life seemed as bizarre as flying to Mars.

Esther patted my hand like I was a baby and told me her e-mail address: esthermacholo@hotmail.com. She whispered that the cafe manager lets her use leftover time on his Internet coupons because he likes her. She winked and showed me her collection of business cards. "They're from the tourists who take my picture," she bragged. "When I'm bored, I send them e-mails. Sometimes they write back. If their friends are coming to town, for instance."

"'If their *friends* are coming to town?'"

"What's wrong with that?"

"Guess."

"It's not like I go to their rooms, or anything. I just stand in front of that fountain and let them take my photo."

"Make sure you keep it that way."

"Meaning?"

"Don't play dumb. I've seen them get down on one knee to look up your skirt."

Esther rolled her eyes. "They go on one knee so the top of the statue will fit in the picture. You and your dirty mind. You're worse than my auntie."

"It's not just me," I pleaded. "Kids at school are talking."

"Let them."

"Look, Esther—"

"No, *you* look, Chanda!" she snapped. "Maybe you want to be stuck in Bonang having babies, but not me. I'm getting out. I'm going to America or Australia or Europe."

"How? You think some tourist is going to put you in his suitcase?"

"No."

"What then? Marry you?"

"Maybe," she said. "Or hire me as a nanny."

I snorted.

"Why not?"

"Because. That's why not."

Esther shot me a look. She got up from the computer, stormed out, and marched across the parking lot.

I ran after her. "Esther!" I shouted. "Stop. I didn't mean it. I'm sorry." I wasn't sorry, but I hate it when we fight. I caught up to her at an abandoned shopping cart. She gripped the bar and stared at an advertising flyer in the basket.

"I know I talk crazy," she said. "It's just... sometimes I like to dream, okay?"

Esther's not in the Internet cafe today. She's not anywhere at the mall, for that matter. Maybe she's running an errand for her auntie. Maybe she's at school for once. Or maybe she's met a tourist and—

I hop on my bike and pedal as fast as I can: ABCDEFG-HIJKLMNOP...

3

HOME WASN'T ALWAYS A SHANTYTOWN IN BONANG.

Our family started out on Papa's cattle post, a spread of grazing land near the village of Tiro, about two hundred miles north. I shared a one-room mud hut with Mama, Papa, an older sister and three older brothers. (There would have been two other sisters, but they died before I was born. One from bad water, one from gangrene.) My aunties, uncles, and cousins also had huts in the compound. My papa-granny used to live there too, but since my papa-grampa died she's stayed in the village with a couple of single aunties.

Life on the cattle post was slow. In winter, the riverbeds dried up and the sparrows' nests hung like straw apples from the acacia trees. All the plants shriveled to the bare ground, and only the mopane trees, and a few jackalberries kept us from being desert. Me and my cousins would spend the days helping our mamas collect well water, or herding the cattle with our papas.

But I also remember how the rains came in summer, the rivers ran and overnight the reeds and grasses would spring up over our heads, and the cattle would graze untended while we played hide-and-seek. The cattle always knew when it was time to return to the enclosure, and how to get there. Us kids weren't so lucky. Getting lost in the grass was easy, so we learned how to recognize the top of each tree for miles around; they were our street signs.

I was little, so I didn't understand why the fighting started. All I knew was that Papa was the youngest of his brothers and he and my uncles quarreled about our share of the harvest. As a result, when the diamond mine here in Bonang expanded, Papa signed up and we came south, except for my older sister Lily, who stayed behind to marry her boyfriend on the neighboring post.

At first I was homesick. I missed playing with my cousins. I also missed the country and the big sky: the way the sun grew fat when it went to bed, sinking below the horizon like a giant flaming orange; or the way the stars turned the night into a canopy of wonders. In the city, the sky closed in, and the magic of the night dwindled in the spill of the light from the mine and the downtown streets.

Still, Bonang had advantages. We had a new home made of cement blocks instead of mud, and there was a standpipe with fresh water on every street. There was also a hospital in case we got sick, and Papa said the company ration cards meant we never had to worry about going hungry. What mattered most to me, though, was that my aunties and uncles couldn't snoop on me. And while I missed my cousins, I made friends with the other miners' kids.

Like Esther. The first day I arrived, I was sitting in my yard feeling lonesome and thinking about running away back to Tiro. That's when Esther skipped up. She had the biggest combs in her hair I'd ever seen. "Hi," she said. "I'm Esther. I'm six."

"I'm Chanda. I'm six, too."

"Hooray, that makes us twins. I've lived here since forever and ever. Watch me get dizzy." She spun around in circles and fell down. "Guess what? My papa's a foreman. We have a flush toilet. Want to see it?" She grabbed me by the hand and yanked me down the road to her house. Her mama was shelling peas on the front stoop when we arrived.

"This is Chanda. I'm showing her our toilet," Esther said, pulling me inside before I had a chance to say "hello."

At first, I couldn't believe that I was looking at a toilet. I thought it was a fancy soup bowl. "Watch this!" Esther crowed. She yanked a chain. There was a roar like a giant waterfall. I screamed.

Esther giggled. "When boys give me a hard time, I tell them I'm going to stuff them in my toilet, and flush them into the river with the crocodiles."

"Can I try it?"

Esther nodded. "But then we have to disappear fast, because Mama will be after us for wasting water."

I yanked the chain, the waterfall roared, and we ran out the back door as Esther's mama came down the corridor yelling, "That's enough flushing, Esther. It's not a toy."

A couple of houses away we collapsed in laughter. "I thought our outhouse was special, with the cement shelf to sit on," I said. "But your toilet—it's like magic! You'll never guess where we had to pee at the cattle post."

"Where?" Esther's eyes danced in anticipation.

I scrunched up my face to make it sound as awful as possible. "In a tiny reed hut. All the women had to squat over a hole in the ground."

"Eaow!" Esther squealed in delight. "What about the men?"

"They peed on the walls!"

"Eaow! Eaow! Eaow!" she shrieked.

"They had to," I roared. "Too much liquid in the hole made the sides collapse."

"And you could fall in!"

"Maybe even drown!"

"EAOWOOOO!!!" We both howled with laughter and rolled around hysterically. I tried to explain that when the reeds got too stinky we threw them away and got new ones, but I couldn't get past the word "stinky" without setting off another explosion of giggles.

Esther and I went to the same school. It wasn't like the cattle post school where I sat under a tree and my aunties taught me how to sew. And it wasn't like my school in the village either—a school with only a blackboard, and a schoolmaster who used hard, white hyena droppings when the chalk ran out. No. This school came with a library, a science lab, geometry kits, a set of encyclopedias, and working pencil sharpeners.

Some of my teachers came from the local university; others, on two-year visas from North America. I "soaked up everything," as Mr. Selalame would say. He's the English teacher I have now, not to mention my favorite teacher of all time. Esther teases me. She thinks I'm sweet on him. I tell her not to be stupid.

It's just, some teachers get mad when I ask them hard questions. Not Mr. Selalame. If he doesn't know the answer, he'll wink and say he'll get back to me. He does, too, not only with the answer but with a book he thinks I'd like. Something by Thomas Mofolo or Noni Jabavu, or Gaele Sobott-Mogwe. I read them as fast as I can so he'll lend me another. Mr. Selalame says if I keep at my studies I could win an overseas scholarship and see the world. The way his eyes light up, I think he really believes it.

"Why wouldn't he believe it?" Mama says when I tell her. "There's nothing you can't do if you set your mind to it."

Mama and Mr. Selalame believe in me so much I get goosebumps. I hope I don't let them down. What they say sounds impossible. But what if they're right? What if I could get a scholarship? See the world? Become a doctor, a lawyer, a teacher? Dreams, dreams, dreams.

My brothers would laugh to hear me talk like that. "Don't get your hopes up," they'd say. "Scholarships and good jobs only go to the rich." They dropped out of school as soon as they could to join Papa underground. Every day a bus would drive them to the mine before dawn and bring them back after dark, or vice versa. They had one day off a week.

Pit-mining can give you lung diseases, but Papa and my brothers didn't live long enough to get sick. Just before I turned ten, a blast misfired and their tunnel caved in. They were among thirty miners who died. There were rumors they suffocated slowly because the company's rescue equipment didn't work. I had nightmares of them gasping to death, until Papa came to me in a dream to say that they died in the explosion—"It was so quick we didn't feel a thing." I tried to talk to him some more, but I woke up. He's never come back.

A week after the funerals, a man from the mine drove by. Mama was hanging laundry. She always used to wipe off a plastic chair for visitors to sit on. But not for him. She just stood there with her hands on her hips.

The man hemmed and hawed: "The company's very sorry for your loss, Mrs. Kabelo."

Mama kept staring.

"Nothing can replace your husband or sons," the man went on, "but the company wants to offer you a little money to get you on your feet again." He gave her an envelope.

Mama threw it at his head. "Blood money!" she said. "You killed my man! You killed my babies! Get out of my yard, you sonofabitch!"

The man scrambled to his car. He yelled that our yard was company land. It was only for miners. Since Papa and my brothers were dead, we'd have to leave or pay rent. Mama threw stones at him as he sped away.

Next day, our ration cards were cut off, and we got an order to pay rent or have our belongings seized. Neither Papa nor my brothers had saved a penny. They hadn't made a will or taken out insurance, either. They thought those things were bad luck. So we had to use the blood money, even though it wasn't much. I thought for sure we'd be heading back to Tiro.

"No," Mama said. "Not even if it's the last place on earth."

"Why not?"

"Because."

"But we could live at Papa's cattle post. Or in the village with Granny Kabelo. Or at Granny and Grampa Thela's. Or with Lily—her husband wouldn't mind, would he? We hardly ever get to see her, and she only has one baby so far and there'd be lots of room."

"Chanda," Mama said sharply, "there're things you don't understand."

"Like what?"

"I'll tell you when you're older."

"But I need to know now. Where are we going to live? How are we going to eat?"

Mama held me close and kissed my forehead. Then out of nowhere she let out a laugh. I'm not sure if it was to make me feel better, or because I looked so serious, or because she didn't know what else to do. All I know is, after she laughed, she rocked me. "Don't you worry," she said. "Mama will figure out something." And she closed her eyes.

I stayed very still, but my mind was racing. Why wouldn't Mama take us back to Tiro? What was the terrible secret she was afraid to tell me?

4

AFTER THE BLOOD MONEY RAN OUT, we couldn't afford to buy meat or eggs, so we stuck to soup and bread. Soon we cut out the bread. That's when Mama said she'd been offered a job cleaning house for Isaac Pheto. He'd left his wife and kids at a village hundreds of miles away to work at the mine. He sent them money on payday.

Isaac's house was like all the other general workers' houses. It had two rooms: a common room with a small kitchen, and a bedroom. He let us sleep for free on an old mattress in the common room. I was told to call him Isaac.

Isaac's place was filthy—even the walls were caked with grime—but Mama soon had it looking nice. She even sewed curtains with material she got from a street seller, bright yellow and blue. And she pummeled his work clothes in an outdoor tub till they smelled like fresh grasses.

Our prayers seemed to be answered. Then one night I woke up and Mama wasn't beside me. I thought maybe she'd gone to the outhouse, but then I heard the sounds coming from Isaac's room. "Shh, she'll hear us." I pretended to be asleep when Mama sneaked back to our bed.

"Do you still think about Papa?" I asked the next morning as she swept the ground in front of the house.

Her shoulders slumped. "All the time," she said. And kept on sweeping.

I knew that Mama knew that I knew. But we didn't talk about it. We both pretended nothing was going on for another week. Then one night, I got up before dawn and sat in a corner. When she tiptoed from his room back to our bed, I lit a candle. We didn't say anything. From then on, she tucked me in, and went to his room directly.

A year later, Iris was born: my first half-sister.

Iris's christening service ran from ten o'clock Sunday morning until four in the afternoon. A neighborhood celebration followed that lasted into the night. Our street didn't have electricity, so we lit a fire in the firepit, and stuck torches in the ground. The neighborhood clapped and danced and sang, and Mama told stories that made everyone howl with laughter. I tried to stay awake, but I was only eleven and fell asleep around midnight.

Next thing I remember, I was in the dark on my mattress. Someone was touching me all over.

"Who's there?"

"Relax," Isaac whispered. "It's only me."

"What are you doing?" I whispered back.

"Tucking you in."

"That's not how Mama does it."

"I'm not your mama. Or your papa. That's why it's different."

I didn't know what to do, so I froze.

"That's a good girl," he said. "Nice and quiet."

The door opened. "Isaac?" It was Mama.

"Lilian!" he jumped back. "Shh. I'm just putting Chanda to bed. Poor thing's fast asleep."

"Oh," Mama whispered. "Well, hurry up. We need you out here for a toast."

"Right away." Isaac followed her out. At the doorway he turned to me and winked. "Sleep tight."

Pretty soon after that, I stopped eating. At first, Mama thought, I had a sick stomach. Then she got worried. "What's the matter?" she asked.

"Nothing."

The truth was, everything was the matter. Since the night of the party, Isaac had been after me. Even in the middle of the night with Mama in the next room. Daytime too. When Mama went to fetch water at the standpipe, he'd say: "Sit on my lap." That's how it would start. I told Mama I wanted to help her with the water, but she always said she needed me to chop carrots, or to keep an eye on the baby.

I wanted to scream what was happening. But I figured he'd just deny it and I'd get in trouble. Even worse, if Mama believed me, she'd say we had to leave—we'd be homeless with nothing to eat and it would be all my fault. Or that's what I thought.

It turned out differently. That afternoon Mama came back from the standpipe early and caught him with his pants down.

"You're not a man! You're a monster! "she screamed. She

heaved the water at him and bashed him over the head with the pail. He threw her across the room.

"Go whore in the streets with your slut daughter!" he yelled, loud enough that the neighbors would hear. Then he grabbed our clothes and threw them out the windows.

Mama stuffed them into a couple of plastic bags. She put Iris on a sling over her shoulder, took the bags in one hand and my hand in her other. "I curse you, Isaac Pheto," she spat at him. "By all that is holy, I curse your name, and the bones of the ancestors who bore you."

The neighbor women were listening to the fight from inside their homes, but some of the men had come out for the show. Mama spiked them with a look. "What are you gawking at, misters?"

She hiked her chin and together we strode down the street. As we were about to turn the corner, I felt the tears coming. "Don't cry, Chanda," Mama whispered calmly. "Never let them see you cry."

Mrs. Tafa took us in. Papa and her first husband had worked the same shift at the mine. They died together in the cave-in. But unlike Mama, Mrs. Tafa had luck. Her brother-in-law married her right after the funeral. He was a bricklayer with The United Construction Company. On his days off, he'd built a row of cement-block rooms on the far side of his yard, which he rented. We didn't have any money left, but Mrs. Tafa said we could stay in one of the rooms until she found a paying boarder.

"Thank you," Mama said, "but we won't be needing charity. In exchange for the room, we can tend your garden, do your chores, and run errands."

Mrs. Tafa agreed.

That night when Mr. Tafa got home from work, he drove Mama back to Isaac's for the rest of our things. We'd left pots, pans, a few sheets and towels, and Iris's toys. Mostly, though, Mama wanted the reminders of Papa and my brothers: their funeral programs and Papa's hunting rifle. "That Isaac Pheto wasn't so brave with your man around," Mama told Mrs. Tafa. "He just hid in a corner and let me take what I came for."

Mr. and Mrs. Tafa didn't have any children together, but they both had kids from their first marriages. The only one at home was Mrs. Tafa's son Emmanuel. He was older than me, and very smart. I hardly ever saw him because he was always studying. Their other kids were all married and would bring their families over on birthdays and feast days, or just for fun.

Whenever they had a celebration, the Tafas made sure that Mama and I were invited. I got to call them Auntie and Uncle.

Next door to the Tafas was a kind old barber named Mr. Dube. He had rotten teeth, but he kept the smell down by gargling hair tonic.

He cut people's hair in an open shed at the side of the road. People came to him from all over the neighborhood, because he was such a great talker and kept his scissors sharp and his combs clean. He also had a set of clippers hooked up to a twelve-volt battery, and a radio so people could dance a bit if they were bored waiting in line.

Mr. Dube was a widower with a house but no children. Mama was a widow with two children and not much else. It didn't take long before he came courting. He wasn't much to look at, but he said Mama's name, "Lilian," hushed and respectful, like it came from the Bible. And he owned his own place, so we wouldn't have to worry about being on the street again. Mama accepted his proposal.

After the wedding, he asked me to call him Papa. I said thank you, but I couldn't, on account of Papa's memory. He smiled gently and said he understood, that "Mr. Dube" would be fine.

My half-brother Solomon, "Soly," was born a year later. He was cute as a dimple. Still is. While I went to school, Mama looked after Iris and Soly while Mr. Dube cut hair and entertained the customers. In the evening, we'd sit together in the front yard and tell stories and laugh. Mama would rub Mr. Dube's swollen feet as he cuddled Iris and Soly. I'd hug my knees and grin.

We were happy like that for a while. Then one night Mr. Dube said he had an upset stomach. He lay down and never got up. It was a stroke. I cried for ages, but I tried to comfort myself that Mr. Dube was lucky. The stroke was sudden and painless. He didn't suffer. I'd like to die like that.

Sometimes I feel guilty about remembering Mr. Dube's rotten teeth. He was so good to all of us. Looking back, I wish I'd been able to call him "papa." My real papa wouldn't have minded. And it would have meant so much to Mr. Dube. I hope he knew I loved him.

Mama inherited the house, which gave us a place to live. She also started a vegetable garden and raised a few chickens in the front yard. But there was no money. Mr. Dube's trips to the herbal doctor, and his funeral, had eaten most of his savings, and now Mama had three of us to support.

I guess that's how Jonah happened. Mama had a house, and

he had a job. He asked Mama to marry him, but she said no. She wanted to keep the ownership of Mr. Dube's property to protect Iris, Soly, and me, in case things didn't work out.

Jonah was a friend of Mr. Tafa's from the construction company. He was a big talker with a great smile, who poured concrete for malls and office buildings downtown. That is, until he got fired. Jonah liked to party and the company got tired of not knowing whether or not he'd show up for work.

When Mama was pregnant with Sara, he was still making some money doing odd jobs. But since Sara's birth and Mama's miscarriages, he's mainly just stayed at the shebeen getting drunk on shake-shake.

That's where he is now, I'll bet.

5

WHEN I GET BACK FROM THE ETERNAL LIGHT, it's ten. Iris and Soly are in the front yard where I left them. Mama said Iris didn't have to go to kindergarten today, so they know something important's happened, only they're not sure what.

Soly sits quietly by the front door playing with his toes. Iris, on the other hand, is in one of her moods. She's marching up and down the yard with a storm cloud over her head. When she sees me, she stalks up and plants her hands on her hips.

"Sara's still sleeping. She's been sleeping all morning. Make her stop."

"Don't be such a bossy brat."

"I'm not," she says, stomping her foot.

"I mean it, Iris. Act your age or I'll smack you."

"Go ahead," she dares me. "I'll tell."

When Iris gets like this, there's no sense arguing. She's too smart for her own good. And mine. "Why don't you water the beans?"

She yawns as if the reason is obvious.

"Fine," I say. "Be bored if you like. I don't care."

Iris sighs. "Get over here, Soly, I have a game. We're going to see who can make the biggest pile of stones. Only they have to come from the front yard, and we can only pick them up with our elbows."

I go into the house. The shutters are open to keep out the death smell.

Mama has braided Sara's hair and laid her on the mattress that she shares with Jonah. She's curled up beside her, stroking her cheek. I tell her about Mr. Bateman coming at one. I leave out the part about the service having to be on Thursday. "Mr. Bateman says not to worry, the funeral will be beautiful."

Mama doesn't look up. "Go back to Mr. Bateman and tell him not to come. We can't pay. Someone's stolen the money from the hiding place."

Mama doesn't say who stole it. She doesn't have to.

"It's not stolen, Mama," I lie, to make her feel better. "I took it to Mr. Bateman for the deposit."

Mama shudders. "God forgive me. Sometimes I think terrible things."

I kiss her on the forehead. "You rest now. I'll be right back."

I run outside, hop on my bike, and head to the local shebeen.

The shebeen is owned and run by the Sibandas. It's a large, open-air booze pit surrounded by a six-foot cement wall that comes up to the dirt road. The wall is so that people can't see which of their neighbors are inside, or how drunk they are.

I enter through the high wooden gate, bringing my bike with me so it won't get stolen. To my right, people are sitting and gambling in the shade of a canvas tarp tied to the tops of three posts and a dead tree. To my left, others line up by a shed where Mrs. Sibanda sells cigarettes, Coke, and fried banana chips.

But the center of attention is at the back of the property. It's here that the Sibandas live with their children, in-laws, and grandchildren in a handful of huts as wobbly as the customers. It's also here that Mr. Sibanda brews his shake-shake, and his clients crowd around, pick fights, and throw up, as they wait for the next tub to be ladled out.

Mr. Sibanda's tubs are as clean as any, but sometimes when he stirs up the sludge with the alcohol, a dead beetle floats to the surface. Also, depending on how hot the weather is, or how long the mabele's been fermenting, a few glugs can knock you sideways.

There's a special buzz right now. Two of Mr. Sibanda's sons have just hauled out a fresh tub. One of his granddaughters is pouring the brew into old juice cartons. The Sibandas have collected them from garbage bins and rinsed them in a pail of water.

As I walk toward the crowd, looking for Jonah, I almost trip over two-year-old Paulo Sibanda. He's wearing nothing but a pair of empty juice cartons and a grin. His feet are shoved into the cartons like they were shoes, only they're bigger than his feet, so he keeps falling over, which makes him laugh.

"Hey, Chanda!" The voice is loud. I turn around. It's Mary. She's propped against one of the shade posts, waving haphazardly. "Heard about Sara... Sorry, old friend."

Everyone is "old friend" to Mary. She knows the whole neighborhood. Or at least the whole neighborhood knows her. She went to school with my oldest brother. Back then, she was popular. She was fun and pretty and could sing and imitate people and wasn't stuck-up or anything.

Now she's twenty-five, and has four kids being raised by her mama. She spends her days going from shebeen to shebeen, looking for free drinks. Whenever I see her, she's wearing the same wool cap, pulled down to hide the scar over her right eyebrow. Today she's wearing a pair of drawstring pajama bottoms; they cover the sores on her legs. After her front teeth were broken, she used to put her hand over her mouth when she talked; now she doesn't bother.

There're rumors that when Mary's passed out, men drag her into an outhouse and have their fun. She made a big scene last year, staggering up and down the streets banging on doors demanding to know who stole her underpants. Luckily for Mary, she never remembers anything. Or pretends that it's all a big joke. Even now, a year later, people come up and say, "Hey, Mary, found your underpants?" Then they laugh. And she laughs with them. I wonder what she's really feeling?

Maybe that's why I don't blow up when I see Jonah's head in her lap. Mary isn't the first woman he's messed with. She won't be the last. Besides, he's so juiced up he couldn't do anything even if he wanted to. His eyes are crusty. He blinks to keep out the flies.

Mary cradles him. "He hurts so much," she says. "All he can say is, 'Sara. Sara.'"

Jonah rocks his head. "Sara," he echoes, from some other world.

"Chanda's here," Mary tells him.

Jonah gets a puzzled look. His eyes drift shut.

Mary sees me staring at a fresh gash on his forehead. "He took a rock an' smashed his head to let the demons out," she whispers.

"He should have smashed harder."

At first Mary can't believe her ears. Then she laughs. "I like you, friend. You always make jokes."

"Do I?" I kick Jonah's leg. He surfaces. "Jonah," I say, "Mr. Bateman is picking up Sara at one. Understand?"

"Sara," he murmurs.

"Right. Sara. One o'clock. Home. Be there."

Jonah nods and passes out. I rifle through his pockets.

Mary focuses fast. "What're you doing?"

"Nothing." I find what I'm looking for. A small wad of cash, minus the elastic that held it together. The money from the hiding place. It's almost all there. I get up to go.

Mary shoves Jonah's head aside and hurls herself to her feet. "Where you going with Jonah's money?" she yells. At the word "money," a circle of drunks forms around us.

"It's for the funeral," I say.

"Says who?" She takes a swing at me and almost falls over.

"Settle down, Mary," I say. "You don't need to fight for drink money. Today Jonah will get all the free drinks he wants."

Mary's arms fall to her sides. She rocks on her feet, laughs, and shakes my hand. "You're a good friend, Chanda. A good friend."

"Right. Just make sure he's home by one."

I shove my bike through the crowd. The crowd backs off, as if people are afraid I'll hit anyone in my way. I will, too.

6

SOMETIMES I GET EVIL THOUGHTS. Just now, for instance. Checking Jonah's pockets, all I could think was: "Jonah, why don't you die? Our lives would be so much easier!" The priest says evil thoughts are as bad as evil deeds. They're something we have to confess. I've been confessing this thought every week for the past two years. It's getting embarrassing.

But really, why is Mama with Jonah? Why couldn't she be with somebody like my teacher, Mr. Selalame? He's so smart, and funny, and kind. Handsome, too. Sometimes I sit in class and imagine him being my papa. Aside from my real papa, he'd be the best papa in the world.

I see him in the market with his family. He and his wife whisper in each other's ears and chuckle, as if they have a private world all to themselves. Once I saw him at a vegetable stand entertaining his son and daughter by juggling five potatoes and a turnip. He can do everything.

The priest says jealousy's another sin, and I have enough sins to confess as it is. So when I catch myself thinking about Mr. Selalame's family, I work hard to remember good things about Jonah. How I didn't always hate him. In fact, how I used to be glad he was with Mama.

Most men don't look twice at a woman who's forty with three children. But Jonah didn't care. From the very beginning, despite everything, he's always loved Mama. He's treated us kids like we were his own, too. When he moved in, Mama started to sing again—just sing for no reason. And for the first time since Papa died, I saw her dance

On his sober days, Jonah can still make Mama glow. He hugs

her, and helps with problems, and plays with Soly and Iris. He works hard, too—fixing up the place, doing odd jobs, and repairing and selling things he collects at the junkyard. Best of all, he makes Mama laugh. I love her laugh. It's stout and strong, like a mama with huge breasts, chubby thighs, and a round belly for babies to bounce on.

Mama used to look like her laugh, but not anymore. She's lost weight worrying about Sara. "I need to put on a few pounds," she'll say when she looks in the mirror. "Don't be silly," Jonah tells her. "You look perfect the way you are." That makes her smile.

When Jonah first moved in, those little things made me like him. Not now. Since Mama's miscarriages, his good days—the sober days—have gotten fewer and fewer. Most nights, his friends ask him out for a drink. He always goes. Once, when Sara had a bad fever, Mama begged him to stay home. She even blocked the doorway. His friends laughed. Jonah said she was shaming him. He smashed some plates to show who was boss and went on a bender for a week.

Esther says I should count my blessings. No matter how drunk Jonah gets, he never hits us. And he always crawls back full of tears and regrets.

"So what?" I said. "When he drinks, he's a whole other person. He falls down, he stinks, and worst of all he cheats on Mama."

"Don't be a baby," Esther said. "Lots of men cheat. All over the world."

"How would you know?"

She got a funny look in her eye. "I just do."

Esther can act all grown-up if she likes. What I know is, if it was anyone else but Jonah, Mama would send him packing. But somehow Jonah gets away with everything. The night he smashed the plates I went crazy. "Why don't you kick him out?" I demanded.

Mama's eyes flashed. "Never say that again, you hear? You're talking about Sara's papa. Show some respect!"

"Why?" I demanded. "He doesn't show any to us."

Mama got very quiet. "I know it's hard. But forgive him. He's in pain."

"Who isn't?"

Mama didn't answer. She knelt down, gathered the bits of plate into her apron, and closed her eyes.

The last few months, while Jonah's been out with his friends, we've stayed up soothing Sara's rashes with a tea of devil's claw root. Whenever I've heard a drunken holler from outside I've jumped up ready to scream. Not Mama. She's never taken her eyes off her work. "Jonah's promised to quit drinking," she says. "He will one day. You'll see."

I know it's important to believe in things. All the same, love makes people stupid.

7

As soon as I get back from the shebeen, I go next door to see Mrs. Tafa. I have to ask her to use the phone to let our relatives know about Sara.

I'm nervous. Mrs. Tafa and I don't get along anymore. I told Mama I wanted to stop calling her "Auntie." Mama said that would hurt her feelings. "Fine," I said, "then I won't call her anything." I don't know if I've changed, or if she's changed, or if I just see her differently.

All I know is, Mrs. Tafa would like to run the world. Since she can't run the world she's decided to run our neighborhood. Especially me and my family. Before the sun gets too hot, she makes a grand tour with her flowered umbrella, a matching cotton hankie up her sleeve. She pretends she's just going around to be sociable, but it's really to tell everyone how to raise their children or plant their vegetables. "If that one was mine," she'll say to a mama whose baby is teething, "I'd have it suck a carrot."

Mrs. Tafa makes a special point to end her travels at our place. Mama's expected to stop her work and fetch her a cup of tea and a biscuit. This is because Mrs. Tafa gave us a place to stay when we were desperate, and because Papa and her first husband were friends, and because we've always been invited to her celebrations. I've asked Mama if that means we're stuck with her forever.

"Hush," Mama laughed. "We're neighbors."

At any rate, Mrs. Tafa sits in the shade of our house, eating, drinking, and daubing her forehead with her hankie, while she fills Mama in on the latest gossip, and makes Soly and Iris fan her.

Luckily I'm at school during the week, but on weekends and holidays I'm expected to join them. I sit on the ground and read a book or do my homework. Mrs. Tafa's such a goat I try to ignore her. But I can't help listening when she and Mama tell stories from when we lived at the mine.

Most of the stories are funny, such as the one about Papa going on night shift after Mama'd fed him three plates of black beans. "Twenty men crammed in that elevator," Mrs. Tafa roars, "and your Joshua passing more gas than a pipeline! Serving black beans before night shift? What were you thinking, girl? My Meeshak was passed out for a week!"

Mama laughs so hard the air shakes. "Speaking about your Meeshak," she exclaims, "remember the time you scrubbed the floors and he marched over them in his workboots? I'll never forget the sight of you chasing him up and down the street with that mop!"

Mama and Mrs. Tafa remember other kinds of stories too. Mama tells about the extra shifts Papa worked so we'd have new clothes when we'd visit our relatives in Tiro: "Joshua made sure our heads were held high." And Mrs. Tafa recalls the millions of toasts he was asked to make at anniversaries, birthdays, street parties, and Independence Day celebrations—not to mention his practical jokes and victories at leg wrestling competitions.

They talk about Papa's bravery too. How he helped Meeshak rescue an old woman trapped in a fire at the town hall. And about his long struggle to help organize a union for the miners. "Those bosses and their damn thugs would've killed to know where the union had its meetings," Mrs. Tafa slaps her knee. "It was your Joshua who kept them in the dark, with his secret code of village songs and bird whistles."

I know all the stories by heart, but I can't hear them enough. Each time I hear them, it's like Papa's alive again.

If only Mrs. Tafa could stick to telling stories. But she can't. She always has to ruin everything. Before leaving, she'll peer around the yard and say: "If you don't mind my saying so..." or, "A word to the wise..." or, "I don't mean to be unkind, but..." Then she'll add something rude about how Mama is dressed, or keeps house, or looks after Iris and Soly and me.

Mama cuts her off with a smile. "Now, Rose," she says, "I thought we agreed not to talk about that."

"I'm only trying to be helpful," Mrs. Tafa protests. Then she hoists herself to her feet, gives her umbrella a twirl, and swings her big fat bum out the gate.

One time I asked Mama why Mrs. Tafa's so mean.

Mama laughed. "She's not mean. She's Mrs. Tafa. Pay no attention. She means well."

I'm sure pigs mean well, too, I thought to myself, but they're still pigs.

Mama caught the look in my eye. "Save your anger to fight injustice. Forgive the rest," she whispered, stroking my cheek. "Remember, everyone has problems. Mrs. Tafa's problem is, she needs to feel important."

Mama's too kind. Mrs. Tafa doesn't *have* a problem: Mrs. Tafa *is* a problem. She's so puffed up on herself, I picture her turning into a hot air balloon and sailing into the sunset. If she floated up to heaven, she'd tell the angels how to clean their clouds. And she's getting worse.

The reason she gets away with it is because she's rich, at least for around here. The Tafas have rented all the rooms that Mr. Tafa built, and on top of that, Mr. Tafa's been promoted to head bricklayer with United Construction. With all the extra money, they've got themselves a phone, electricity, and running water.

Mrs. Tafa brags about how her husband gets to go on the Internet with his company's computer, and how they send e-mails to friends and relatives who've emigrated to North America and Europe. As if this isn't enough, Mrs. Tafa has hired a cleaning lady who comes once a week. She says that organizing her cleaning lady is exhausting. But the truth is that all Mrs. Tafa does is sit on her lawn chair and drink lemonade. I hope she drinks so much she gets stuck there.

The priest says that thinking hard thoughts hurts the person who thinks them. All the same, it's hard not to think hard thoughts about someone who's rich and pushes everyone else around. Especially when that someone is Mrs. Tafa.

As I come through the gate, Mrs. Tafa is sitting under a tree on her lawn chair, with a pillow plumped behind her back. Her daughter's dropped off some grandkids. They sit at her feet gulping juice from plastic cups. The oldest fans her with an oversized fly swatter. Iris and Soly are watching through the cactus fence that separates our yards.

Mrs. Tafa hollers a greeting: "Dumêla!"

"Dumêla," I say back. I nod to her grandkids: "Dumêlang."

Mrs. Tafa doesn't bother getting up, just points to the bench opposite her. "I dropped by this morning," she says, "but no one would open your door."

"I'm sorry." I sit. "Something awful's happened."

"So I hear." I'm not surprised she's heard. She has the ears of an elephant.

I glare at Iris and Soly. "Stop eavesdropping. Go pile stones." They do. "Mama doesn't want them to know," I whisper.

"She's right," Mrs. Tafa nods approvingly. "There's no need to involve little ones with things like that." She shoos her grandchildren away. "So... you want to use my telephone?"

"If it's all right, yes, please. I need to let Mama's people know."

"It's your mama who should call."

"She wants to stay with Sara."

"I see." A pause. Mrs. Tafa stretches her arms and wobbles the flab. "A lot of folks want to use my telephone," she says at last. "If I let everyone use it, I'd never get any peace." She tilts her head and wipes the dribbles of sweat from under her chins.

"I know, and I'm sorry for bothering you." I take a deep breath. "It's just... I hoped you wouldn't mind... you being my 'Auntie' Rose."

Mrs. Tafa smiles. She sucks the end of her lemonade through a straw. "Who's doing the arrangements?"

"Mr. Bateman."

"Ah." The way she says "Ah" makes me feel like dirt.

"I tried the other mortuaries," I lie, "but they were full up."

"No need for excuses. People will understand," Mrs. Tafa says. "Besides, Mr. Bateman did up the Moses boy, no complaints. All the same, you should have come to me. I have connections."

"Sorry, Auntie." I shift in my seat. "So, about your telephone...?"

"How many calls do you want to make?"

"Just one. To the general dealer in Tiro. He can get the word to my mama-granny, Granny Thela. She'll see to the rest."

Mrs. Tafa sucks her teeth. "Tiro. That's two hundred miles away. Calls to Tiro don't come cheap."

"Mama will pay you back."

Mrs. Tafa waves her hand. "Don't be silly. I'm your auntie. Glad to help." She heaves her rump out of the chair and leads me into her house.

While I wait for the operator to connect me, "Auntie" dusts the shrine on the nearby side table. It's to her youngest son, Emmanuel: his baptismal certificate, undergraduate photograph from university, funeral program, and an envelope of baby hair. Emmanuel died two years ago in a freak hunting accident, just weeks after winning a scholarship to study law in Jo'burg. It was a closed casket. Life isn't fair.

The general dealer, Mr. Kamwendo, answers his phone. Mrs. Tafa kneels by Emmanuel's photograph and pretends to pray, but I can tell she's listening in.

I explain to the dealer about Sara's death and how the burial is set for Thursday. Mr. Kamwendo says he'll pass on the news to my mama-granny and asks if the family can call us at this number. I interrupt Mrs. Tafa's prayers to check. She sighs heavily, but I can tell she's happy as a cow dropping pies: she'll get to hear our news firsthand.

I hang up. Mrs. Tafa struggles to her feet, escorts me back outside, and drops into her lawn chair.

"Thanks again for the use of your phone, Auntie," I say. I lower my head. She gives it a peck. For a second I try to like her.

"Your dear little Sara," she comforts. "Her death's a great tragedy, like my blessèd Emmanuel's. At least they died pure."

My legs go hollow. "Pardon?"

"They were innocents. No one can spread rumors about why they died. No one can point fingers at our families and whisper." She taps her nose. "If you don't mind me saying so, you be careful around that Esther Macholo friend of yours."

"What do you mean?"

"May her parents rest in peace, but I hope she burned their sheets and buried their dishes."

"How can you say that?"

"I don't mean to be unkind," she cautions, "but I keep an ear out."

"There's nothing wrong with Esther. Her mama died of cancer. Her papa died of TB. They died like they said at the funerals."

"Of course they did, and you didn't hear any different from me. Your auntie just wants to protect you, that's all." She winks slyly. "A word to the wise: there's what people said, and there's what people say."

"I don't know what you're talking about."

"Oh, yes, you do," she whispers. "Oh, yes, you do."

8

MRS. TAFA IS RIGHT. I *do* know what she's talking about. New cemeteries overflow as fast as they open. Officially it's because of pneumonia, TB, and cancer. But that's a lie, and everyone knows it.

The real reason the dead are piling up is because of something else. A disease too scary to name out loud. If people say you have it, you can lose your job. Your family can kick you out. You can die on the street alone. So you live in silence, hiding behind the curtain. Not just to protect yourself, but to protect the ones you love, and the good name of your ancestors. Dying is awful. But even worse is dying alone in fear and shame with a lie.

Thank god nobody whispered "AIDS" when Esther's parents got sick. Her papa had a cough and her mama had a bruise. It started as simply as that.

At first, Mrs. Macholo's bruise was so small I hardly noticed it. It was months before I realized it hadn't gone away. It had gotten bigger, darker—and more bruises had started to appear. Before I knew what was happening, Mrs. Macholo was covering her arms and legs with heavy shawls and long skirts.

At the same time, Mr. Macholo's cough got worse. Some days his lungs had a dry rattle. Other days they gurgled like they were full of thick soup. He'd heave up wads of mucous into a china bowl, hacking so fierce I thought his lungs would rip themselves inside out.

I was visiting Esther the day of his last attack. We screamed for help as he thrashed around the floor gasping, choking, for what seemed like forever. He drowned in his own retch.

Esther's mama fell apart. It was as if she'd stayed alive to take care of him. Now she lay in bed refusing to eat.

"There's a tumor at her temple the size of an egg," Esther wept. "It's growing into her brain. She's half-blind, sometimes crazy. She doesn't know where she is anymore. She doesn't even know I'm there."

Esther stayed home from school to look after her. I'd bike over at lunch to help. One day the street was full of gawkers. Mrs. Macholo was staggering around the front yard, swinging a rake, screaming that lions were eating her. It took me, Esther, and three neighbors to get her inside.

Esther shoved the neighbors out when the doctor arrived.

"It's the devil come to get me," her mama screamed. Then she burst into tongues.

The doctor sedated her and gave her an examination, while Esther and I huddled with her brothers and sister on the floor of the main room. When the doctor came out of the bedroom, he pulled me and Esther aside. He thought I was family. Esther didn't correct him.

"Nothing can be done," he said. "I'm sorry. I'd like to offer a bed at the hospital, but we're full. Someone needs to be with her full-time, to take her to the toilet, wipe her, bathe her... Do you have an auntie who could stay here for a few weeks?"

"I don't know," Esther said.

"Painkillers will have to be rationed," the doctor continued. "I'll arrange for a harness. She'll need to be restrained. I'll also arrange for some bleach and a box of rubber gloves. You'll all have to wear them when handling her."

"She's our mama," Esther said. "We won't treat her like garbage."

"It's for your own protection. There'll be body fluids. Feces."

"Who cares? We'll wash our hands. You can't catch cancer from germs."

The doctor paused. "I think this is more than cancer. I want to do a test for the HIV/AIDS virus. You and your brothers and sister should have one too."

"No," said Esther, terrified.

"It's best to know the truth."

"Don't insult my mama. Don't insult my family."

"I'm not insulting anyone."

"Yes, you are." Esther raised her fists. "You're saying my family is dirty. That my papa cheated. Or Mama's a drug addict."

"I'm saying nothing of the kind."

"Then how could she have the virus?"

"Miss Macholo," the doctor protested, "I only care about *what* she has. Not how she got it."

"Get out of here," Esther screamed. "Get out of here now."

When the doctor left, Esther looked at me in horror.

"Don't worry," I whispered. "I won't say a word."

I kept my promise. I acted like everything was normal. Maybe it was, for all I knew. Cancer is cancer, and lots of miners get TB. That's what everyone said at the burial feast. In the words of the priest, "Death tiptoed through the door when no one was watching. It could happen to anyone."

Each month since Mrs. Macholo's funeral I've breathed easier. By now, I was certain Esther was safe behind the curtain. But if Mrs. Tafa is whispering, how many other whispers are in the wind, spreading like germs, infecting minds? How soon before the curtain blows open? And then what?

I leave Mrs. Tafa's yard with an extra swing in my step, so she won't know how much she's upset me. Iris and Soly are crouched at the side of the road in front of our place.

"What are you doing?"

"Looking at ants," Iris says without looking up. "They're pulling a dead fly."

Soly nods. "It's a parade."

"It's not a parade," Iris corrects. "It's a funeral. They're taking him to the fly cemetery to bury him."

"That's no fun. I say it's a parade."

Iris glares at him. She picks up the fly by a wing and shakes off the ants. Then she heads down the road with Soly in pursuit. "There's no parade. We're having a funeral. Understand? I'm the priest, I get to say prayers. You're a mourner, you get to cry."

I leave them arguing and turn into our yard. My heart stops. Esther is lying on the ground by the cactus hedge, her bicycle on one side of her, her school bag on the other. She must have arrived while I was inside Mrs. Tafa's.

Why is it that people always show up when you're talking about them? It's like they're ants with antennae that can pick up their names from miles away.

"Dumêla!" I call out as I approach.

Esther gets up, rubs her eyes, and waves. The bracelets on her arm flash sunlight. "I came as soon as I heard," she says, and hugs me.

Back in her lawn chair, Mrs. Tafa sends us the evil eye.

"Let's go for a walk," I say.

We head arm in arm to the park. All the way I'm thinking: How much did she hear? Was she asleep when Mrs. Tafa attacked her family?

The park is an empty sandlot with a few patches of weeds, a set of swings, and a teeter-totter. We sit on the swings and twirl around until the chains are knotted up. Then we take our feet off the ground and spin. Esther laughs. She still likes to get dizzy.

When the swings are still, we stare at the ground, scuffing our toes in the sand.

"Chanda," Esther says at last, "you know I'll always be your friend, right?"

"Right."

"I mean, even if people say awful things about your family ... even then I'll be your friend."

I feel a chill. "What are people saying?"

"Nothing. But if they ever do." An awkward pause. Then Esther says, "What if people spread rumors about *my* family?"

"Pardon?"

"You heard me. If people spread rumors about *my* family, would you still be my friend?"

I try not to blink. But the way she says it, I know two things. Esther heard everything Mrs. Tafa said. And what Mrs. Tafa hinted is true.

So what? I think. Deep down, I already guessed her parents had AIDS. So nothing's changed. But if nothing's changed, why am I scared?

"Tell me," she presses. "Would you still be my friend?"

"Stop talking crazy. It's bad luck."

"Answer my question."

I know the facts from school. You can only catch AIDS from blood and semen. All the same, if people say you have it you can be shunned. Your family and friends can be shunned, too.

Esther gets off her swing and comes toward me. "Would you still be my friend or not?"

I jump up and back away. Her eyes fill with tears. She turns and starts to run.

"Wait!" I catch up to her, whirl her around, hug her, and plant a kiss on both cheeks. "Of course I'd still be your friend. Your best friend."

Esther squeezes me hard. "I knew you'd say that," she laughs. "We're best friends forever. No matter what, you'll never let me down. I knew it!"

But the truth is, she didn't.

And until right now, neither did I.

9

MAMA IS WAITING AT THE ROAD when Esther and I get back. She whispers that she wants Iris and Soly to be away when Mr. Bateman comes. Esther offers to take them downtown to the YMCA lunch counter for some seswa and a Coke.

When they get the news, Iris and Soly practically do somersaults. They think bus rides are the biggest adventure in the world. And they love Esther. She lets them wear her costume jewelry. It may be fake, but they don't care. It's bright and colorful, and they spend whole days pretending they're kings and queens, or acting out legends I bring home from Mr. Selalame's English class.

I give Esther a few extra coins and tell her to take them to the bazaar afterwards; one of the street sellers might have a little toy to keep them busy over the next few days, or a couple of rings to have for their very own.

Once they're gone, Mama goes back to Sara, and I start to prepare soup stock for supper. I put two pails in the wheelbarrow and go to the standpipe to fetch water. The lineup isn't too bad. People have heard about Sara and say a few words of sympathy.

When I get back, I make a small fire in the pit, fill the pot with water, toss in a few bones and root vegetables, add a little dried chicken meat hanging from the wire by the kitchen window, and set the pot over the fire to simmer for the afternoon. Then I rake the dirt by the front door, so everything will be nice when Mr. Bateman gets here.

After that, there's nothing to do but sit on a stool and wait.

Mr. Bateman arrives at one-thirty. I run to his car and slip him his money. "Sorry I'm late," he says. "I got held up by a last-minute client."

He's not the only one who's late. Jonah still isn't back. Am I surprised?

Mama greets Mr. Bateman at the door and takes him to the bedroom. Sara is laid out in her good dress. She's holding a flower from the garden. She looks so tiny and cold.

"What a dear, sweet thing," Mr. Bateman says. "It's such a pity."

He wraps Sara in a thin cotton sheet, sews the sides together with a loose stitch, and writes a number across the center with gray chalk. "We'll take good care of her," he promises. "You can pick her up at three, day after tomorrow."

Mama nods silently. She kisses the bundle, and watches Mr. Bateman lay it in the back seat of his car. As he drives down the road, she waves good-bye. When the car turns the corner, she stands there, lost.

"Mama?" I whisper. I want to hold her, but she raises a hand and shuts her eyes. A deep breath, and her eyes open. Staring into space, she wanders into the house and closes the door. Inside, I can hear her howling.

Iris and Soly arrive home with yellow tin rings and a new toy. It's a coat hanger bent into a square with pop cans for wheels. Soly insists it's a truck. Iris insists it's a bus.

I invite Esther to stay for supper, but she says she better get back to her auntie's or she'll get a beating. We hug and she bikes off, promising to return Wednesday to help cook the burial feast.

Once she's left, I lift the soup and we gather around the table for supper. Mama's eyes are closed. Iris and Soly pretend not to notice. They've gotten very quiet since coming back.

"What's the matter?" I ask.

Iris stares at her spoon. "Where's Sara?"

I look to Mama for an answer. She doesn't move.

"Sara's gone on a trip," I say carefully. I see Mama nod slightly.

A pause.

Iris frowns. "Why didn't we get to go with her?"

"You were on a trip with Esther."

"Oh."

Another pause.

From Soly, "When's she coming back?"

"You're awful nosy," I say. "Did you like the bus ride downtown?"

"It was okay." They start to fidget, full of questions, but it's clear nobody's going to answer them. It's also clear that they aren't really sure they *want* an answer.

We watch our soup get cold. Finally I get up and pour our bowls back into the pot. "Supper's over," I say.

Iris and Soly drift into a corner and play with their toy. I do the dishes, light the lamps, and change the bedding on the mattress where Sara lay. Then I settle down to try to read my book for English class. Only the words won't stay still; they swim off the page until I'm all mixed up.

Iris tugs at my elbow, Soly beside her. "What's wrong with Mama?" she whispers. I look over. Mama's still at the table with her eyes closed.

"Mama's fine," I whisper back. "She's just thinking, that's all." Iris isn't convinced. "You've seen Mama thinking before," I tell her.

"Not like this."

"Tonight she's just got more to think about, is all."

"Like about what?"

"Like about things that are none of your business." I stroke her cheek. "Don't worry. Everything's fine. Mama won't be thinking much longer."

I'm right, too. There's a sudden rapping at the front.

"Ko ko, it's only me," Mrs. Tafa calls from outside.

Mama's eyes snap open. She taps the hollows of her cheeks, squares her shoulders, and answers the door.

Mrs. Tafa gives Mama a big hug. "So you're finally up for visitors!" She cups a hand to Mama's ear. "Oh, Lilian, I know what it's like, losing a child. When my Emmanuel passed, I wanted to throw myself into the grave with him." She steps back. "At any rate, I won't keep you. Just wanted to let you know, your relatives have phoned from Tiro."

"I'll be right over," Mama says.

"No need. I took a message," Mrs. Tafa beams. "After all, what are friends for?" She waltzes past Mama and plunks herself down at the table. "Your sister Lizbet will be representing the family. She'll be down on tomorrow's bus. The rest of your brothers and sisters send their love and regrets, but they can't make it, it being such short notice, and no one to look after the cattle. Now what am I forgetting?" She taps her head. "Oh yes, your daughter Lily and her husband wanted to come, but Lily's belly is full—congratulations—and she's afraid she might give birth en route, the roads being how they are. And your mama's taking care of your papa. He's laid up in bed with bad bones, but you're not to worry."

She pours herself a glass of water. "All the same," she continues, "they want to contribute to the feast. They're sending sacks of cornmeal, onions, carrots, and potatoes with Lizbet. Also salt. They expect your man is providing the cow. Oh, and by the way, who's Tuelo Malunga?"

"A family friend," Mama says tightly.

"Well, your papa says, 'Tell Lilian, Tuelo Malunga sends his condolences too. Also tell her how he and his wife have just had their eighth boy.' All boys in that family, your papa says. He must be quite the man, that Tuelo Malunga."

"Papa always thought so."

Mrs. Tafa glances at Iris and Soly. "By the way," she whispers, "have you found a place to put the little ones during the you-know-what?"

"Jonah's sister Ruth will take them in, most likely."

"Good." She hesitates. "I don't mean to be unkind, but where is Jonah?"

By the time Mrs. Tafa leaves, we all have headaches. At least her visit's brought Mama back to normal. She pats Iris and Soly on the head and tells them to do their bedtime business. After they've cleaned their teeth, gone to the outhouse, and washed their hands, she tucks them under their sheet.

Iris won't let go of her arm. Her bluster's disappeared.

"What's the matter?" Mama says.

"Nothing," she answers.

Mama rubs noses. "Can you tell me about this nothing?"

Iris trembles. "Did you give Sara away?"

"Yes," Soly echoes. "Did you? Are you going to give us away too?"

"How could you think such a thing?"

"B-because you told Mrs. Tafa we'd be taken in by Auntie Ruth."

Mama shakes her head. "You weren't supposed to hear that."

"But we did," they sob. "Please don't give us away! Please, Mama!"

"Nobody's giving anyone away," Mama says firmly. She hugs them close. "Sara's on a trip, that's all. Auntie Ruth's having you for two days only, because there'll be lots of grownups around here, and you'd be bored."

"No, we wouldn't."

"Yes, you would. At Auntie Ruth's you'll have cousins to play with, and before you know it, you'll be back home with Chanda and me." A pause. "All right?"

The whimpers subside. Iris says, "Will you sleep with us tonight, Mama? Please."

"Of course." She kisses both of them on the hair. "I love you. Don't you ever forget that."

As Mama gets up to finish her chores, Iris looks her in the eye. In a clear, still voice, she says, "Is Sara's trip like the one Soly's papa went on?"

Mama takes a deep breath. "Yes."

There is a long silence. No one cries. Mama and I leave quietly. At the door, I hear Soly whisper, "Iris... will we ever see Sara again?"

"Yes," Iris whispers earnestly. "One day, one day the world will disappear, and we'll all be together again. Sara and your papa and Chanda's papa and everybody. They're making a place for us right now."

"Where?"

"It's a secret."

"But where?"

"In the most beautiful place you can ever imagine."

"Where's that?"

"You'll find out when you're older," Iris whispers, like a mama.

"I want to know now."

"Too bad." Her mama voice disappears. "Go to sleep."

"Not till you tell me where. Wheeeerrrre? Where-where-where-where-where???"

"Go to sleep or else."

"Or else what?"

Iris pokes him. He giggles. She pokes him hard.

"Ow."

"What's going on in there?" I ask in my stern older-sister voice.

"Nothing," from the two of them. A moment of silence, till they think I'm gone. Then giggles, sounds of "Shhh!" and in a moment, everything falls still.

I wake up in the middle of the night. There's a ruckus in the front yard, loud singing, curses, a kicked can clatters against the wheelbarrow. Jonah's friends have brought him home for the night. They toss him toward the house and run.

Jonah staggers to the door. He's too drunk to lift the latch. He slobbers a few words and slides unconscious to the ground. By the light of the moon, I see Mama across the room, lying next to Iris and Soly. Her eyes are open. She's staring at the ceiling.

Most nights, I'd help her drag Jonah inside. I'd flop him on their mattress and leave her to take care of his boots.

Mama says I shouldn't judge Jonah, that he has reasons for why he drinks. Maybe he does. But right now, I don't particularly care what they are. Neither does Mama. We lie in bed, and listen to him snore.

10

THE BUS FROM TIRO IS REALLY A PICKUP TRUCK. It stops wherever people flag it down, and drops them off wherever they're going. Tuesday is normally a quiet day for travel, and we expected Auntie Lizbet in the early afternoon. She arrives after dark with her satchel and three sacks of vegetables.

"The truck ran out of gas. We were stuck for hours while the driver hitched to the nearest garage on a mule cart. Dear lord, and me already seasick from being bounced around all day on top of your onions." She collapses. "I can't walk. You'll have to carry me. And I'll be needing some ice for my lower back."

Mama and I cross our arms and hold hands. Auntie Lizbet wiggles aboard. She clutches our shoulders and we haul her indoors to the rocking chair. While she continues to whine, I bring in the sacks and her satchel, and Mama takes a hammer to the block of ice in the icebox. Mama wraps the chunks in a tea towel, puts the towel in a plastic grocery bag, and tucks it behind Auntie's tailbone.

"Aee! Aee!" Auntie wails.

If it was anyone but her, I'd feel sorry. As it is, I want to laugh.

Iris and Soly are smart enough to stay in their room pretending to sleep, but Jonah sticks his head out of the bedroom. He's been hungover all day with the dry heaves. Mama tries to get him back to bed, but he insists on publicly begging her forgiveness. "I'll never touch a drop again. I swear."

Auntie Lizbet raises an eyebrow. "So you're the new one."

We go to bed. Nobody sleeps, except for Auntie. "Wakey, wakey," she crows bright and early the next morning. With her around, who needs a rooster?

I rub my eyes. It's Wednesday. Two days ago, Sara was alive. Today she'll be home for the laying over. Tomorrow we put her in the ground.

Auntie Ruth arrives at nine for Iris and Soly. She and Jonah have a pleasant conversation, which is surprising considering that the last time he was at her place he tried to steal her jewelry. In addition to babysitting, Auntie Ruth's arranged the meat for tomorrow's burial feast. Jonah's family wouldn't pay for a cow, but she shamed them into contributing two goats. I hope it's enough.

As Soly and Iris leave, Esther arrives to help out. A load lifts from my heart. And the work begins.

Bateman's has provided an open-air tent for visitors staying the night. Mr. Tafa and his male lodgers raise it in the front yard near the cooking pit. Meanwhile Mama, me, Esther, Mrs. Tafa, and Auntie Lizbet get down to cleaning. It's important the house be spotless for Sara's last visit. We start by moving all the furniture and belongings out back.

In less than two trips Mrs. Tafa has worked up a sweat and Auntie Lizbet's griping about her back. They take a break, sipping lemonade and gossiping for the rest of the morning. Esther is a major topic of conversation. At first they whisper in each other's ears, but pretty soon they're being rude right out loud.

"Those are quite the bracelets," Auntie Lizbet hoots to Mrs. Tafa as Esther passes, hauling a chair. "They're so big I'm surprised she doesn't get bruises."

"That's the least of her worries," Mrs. Tafa roars. "If she bends over she'll be showing her panties to the neighborhood." She and Auntie Lizbet laugh so hard they almost fall out of their chairs.

Esther stops in her tracks. She sets down the chair, faces them, and sticks out a hip. "Don't worry, Mrs. Tafa," she smiles sweetly. "I won't be showing off my panties. I'm not wearing any."

"You shouldn't say things like that," I whisper to Esther at the back of the house. "They'll spread it around as if it's true."

Sure enough, on my way back, their tongues are flapping.

"She's always been wild, that one," I hear Mrs. Tafa cluck. "A bad influence. I've warned Lilian."

"Where's her mama?" asks Auntie Lizbet.

"Dead." Mrs. Tafa taps her nose.

Auntie Lizbet squints. "So that explains it."

I want to say something, but what? I'd only make things worse. Luckily the house is now empty. Esther and I can clean inside and pretend they don't exist.

Together with Mama, we scrub down the floors and walls. We also wash all of the cutlery, plates, and cups that the neighbors have lent us for the feast. It arrived clean, but it never hurts to be careful. Then we haul enough wood to the cooking pit to make sure there'll be coals under the stew pots through the night.

Mrs. Tafa and Auntie Lizbet join us for lunch.

"Not bad," says Mrs. Tafa, having a look around. "I don't mean to criticize, but you missed a few spots on the kitchen wall. I'm sure nobody else would notice."

"Oh, I did," says Auntie Lizbet. "And if you ask me, the furniture out back might be lined up more neatly, too. All the same, I suppose I've seen worse."

We ignore them and get changed. Mama suggests I loan Esther a long skirt. I'm embarrassed to suggest it, but Esther doesn't complain. She even volunteers to remove some bracelets and a rhinestone broach.

Then we leave for the Eternal Light.

The moment we arrive, Auntie Lizbet notes the cement mixers next door. "How handy," she says, nodding at Mr. Bateman's patio of pink and gray paving stones.

Today the patio's covered in folding chairs. We sit in the shade of a plastic awning, surrounded by other bereaved families. They come from all sorts of churches. Most have colorful costumes: bright cotton robes and tambourines. Sometimes we join in their singing, but mostly we sit tight in our blacks and navies, like shabby crows at a parade.

Mr. Bateman starts releasing the bodies at three. As he calls out each name, there's a clatter of folding chairs and a gust of clapping and song.

Finally, Sara's name is called. Esther gives my hand a squeeze. I hold my breath and try not to think about what's happening.

Mr. Bateman leads Mama, Jonah, me, and our priest down the corridor, past the coffin showroom, and into a tiny chapel. I'm out of my body somewhere, as he presents Sara in her coffin. She looks so strange. The powder has smoothed where the rash crossed her nose, and they've wrapped the shroud to cover the eruptions on her ears and the bald patches on her scalp. They've also stuffed her cheeks before sewing the lips. I suddenly realize how much weight she'd lost.

Others are filing in now, crowding around us: Esther, Auntie Lizbet, Mrs. Tafa, and Jonah's relatives. I hear a tape of religious music, the priest saying a prayer—and before I know what's happening, Sara is wheeled out the door and the room is following. We pass the embalming station and turn right. Heavy double doors swing open and we're outside in the back parking lot. Sara's placed in a miniature trailer shaped like a coffin, hooked up to a Chevy.

My ears fill with the sound of church ladies singing and banging their tambourines as Mr. Bateman ushers me into the Chevy with Mama and Jonah. Heading out of the driveway, I see a mist of faces: the faces of those who came for Sara, and the faces of the families and friends who've come for the others.

I have a vision. One day there'll be faces come for Mama and for me and for Esther, and Soly and Iris and everyone I love.

I want to bury my head in Mama's breast and scream, "I don't want to die! Why are we born?"

11

THE CHEVY PULLS UP AT OUR HOME, at the head of a convoy of mourners. Two of Jonah's brothers-in-law bring Sara's coffin inside. They take it into the main room and set it on an ironing board. The ironing board is draped in a clean, white bedsheet with Sara's toys spread around the bottom.

Mr. Bateman has provided two plastic wreaths, which Mrs. Tafa insists should stay in their cellophane wrappers to keep clean. She says this is how they do it at the white cemetery. Mrs. Tafa is an idiot, but Mama doesn't argue. She just waits to unwrap them till Mrs. Tafa's gone outside. From now until tomorrow morning only immediate family are allowed inside; by the next time Mrs. Tafa sees the wreaths, she'll have forgotten her advice. Like Mama says, she just likes to be important.

Mr. Bateman circulates, shaking hands and passing out his business card. Neighbors wander up with questions. "We offer a full service," he confides. "There's nothing for you to worry about. We even put a picture of your loved one on the funeral program. If you don't have one, we can take a Polaroid." He gives them a couple of extra cards to give to friends: "It pays to make these plans in advance. Takes away the stress of last-minute decisions."

Meanwhile, Esther prepares the fire and Jonah's sisters chop vegetables, while the goats are brought in from slaughter. They've already been bled. I'm glad. I hate the sound of the squeals, the sight of the dripping, and the smell of the blood that misses the vats and bakes in the ground for weeks.

Mama and I go inside to be with Sara. At the foot of the ironing board, she suddenly clutches her middle and falls to the floor sobbing. I'm scared. This is the first time Mama's ever cried in front of me.

"I'm sorry," she says.

"It's all right. I'm not a baby." The next thing I know I'm on the floor beside her, crying too. We hold each other, gasping for air. When we can breathe again, we wipe our eyes.

"I suppose it's fine to cry in here, just the two of us," Mama says. "But be careful when we welcome visitors."

I nod and do as she says. All afternoon we put on a calm face in public, then come inside to howl.

Most of our friends and neighbors have brought along a sweater, a pillow, and a mat. They'll be sleeping over outside. Esther helps me organize their stuff. My school friends say nice things about Sara, but when Esther sees my lip start to quiver she changes the topic to other things, such as rumors about our teachers. "Two years is a long time for Mr. Joy to spend his nights all alone with history essays," she winks.

For a second I forget the funeral is tomorrow and I laugh. Then new people arrive. "I'm so sorry," they say, and my heart's in my mouth again. I nod my head, shake their hands, say, "Thank you for coming," and run back inside.

Hearing "I'm sorry" is nice. What I hate is: "It's for the best. Sara's with God." I want to say, "If being with God's for the best, why don't you go kill yourself?" I also hate, "Trust God. He has a reason." I want to say, "Oh? Is it the same reason He made you stupid and ugly?"

Thinking those things makes me feel guilty. I want Sara to be with God. I want to believe He has reasons for things. But more than anything, I want Sara alive. I can't stand that she's dead. And I hate people trying to make me feel good about it.

Mrs. Tafa is the worst. While we waited at Bateman's, she leaned over to Mama and said: "Take comfort, Lilian. The poor thing's out of her misery."

"The poor thing?" I wanted to hit her.

Then a terrible thought. What if she was right? Sara suffered from the minute she was born. She cried so much, sometimes I forgot she was my sister. I'd think of her as this horrible screeching thing. She had colic. Running sores and rashes, too. It hurt her to move, so she didn't: she never walked, she barely crawled— a few feeble kicks and fussing, that's all. Mama and I sang to her and told her stories. She hardly ever listened. Hardly ever talked either. Did the fevers affect her brain? Or was talking too painful because of the blisters on her mouth and throat?

I don't know. Nobody knew. Not even the doctors. At least not according to Mama. Early on she took Sara to the hospital. She came home looking like a ghost. She said the doctors couldn't help, they didn't know anything. She never went back.

It was awful. A couple of times I prayed that Sara would die so the crying would stop. Then I slapped myself to make the evil thoughts go away. Now I wonder—did God answer my prayers? Is Sara's death my fault? I don't know what to think—or what I thought—or what I should have thought. I don't even know what I feel.

I wander around lost and confused.

Esther tugs my elbow. "Mr. Selalame's here."

Mr. Selalame? I look over. He's walking towards me. I never dreamed he'd come. He's important, a teacher; I'm just a student.

As Mr. Selalame gives me a hug, his wife comes up beside us.

She hugs me too. It's like we know each other without having met.

The Selalames stay with me while the sun sets. Mama appears. The offer their condolences and she thanks them for coming.

"Chanda's one of my favorite students," Mr. Selalame says. "You must be very proud of her."

Mama beams. My heart swells as big as the world.

The sky glows orange and purple. Torches are lit throughout the yard, and our gathering shakes off its gloom. There are pop cans in a cooler, but some folks nip out to the Sibandas' shebeen. By ten o'clock the night is alive with singing and dancing. Songs from the villages played by old men on the segaba. And best of all, reggae and hip-hop from the Lesoles' boom box.

Mr. Lesole got his boom box with tips from his job as a cook in a safari camp up north. The neighborhood knows whenever he's home on break, because the boom box thumps till all hours, and the street by his yard jumps with parties. Sometimes the noise keeps me awake, but the music brings such cheer, and tonight it's just what we need.

Friends moving with the music cluster in groups all over the yard. They catch up on each other's news, or spread Mrs. Tafa's gossip, or argue with Mr. Nylo the ragpicker about how to choose the best odds and ends for mats.

By midnight, the goats are off the spit, simmering in stewpots. It's then that I see Mary by the road, wool cap pulled extra low as if she's in disguise. She's gripping the hedge to keep her balance, so drunk she doesn't feel the cactus needles. She waves a hip flask to get Jonah's attention. He inches her way.

I tell two of his brothers-in-law to keep an eye on him, but they're into the booze, too. Mary runs off with the three of them.

Jonah's sisters form a posse. They track them to the Sibandas and drag them back by the ears.

About two in the morning, things start to wind down. Some folks sleep under the open tent, but most lie out under the stars. Jonah is stuck in the house under threat of a beating by his sisters, who post themselves at the front door. He stays alone in his bedroom while Mama and I lie awake in the main room with Sara.

Unfortunately, one of Jonah's friends slips him drinks through the window. Just before dawn, we find him with five empty cartons of shake-shake, passed out in his own vomit. We barely manage to clean him up by the time Mr. Bateman arrives with the priest.

Outside the air is as crisp as the sunrise. Most of the gathering have slept well. They rub the night from their eyes and say their "good mornings." The priest officially opens our home, and they file inside and past the open coffin.

Back in the yard, everyone sorts themselves into the backs of pickup trucks. Auntie Lizbet and Mrs. Tafa are staying behind to bake the bread. Esther volunteers to help, but Mrs. Tafa says she'd just be in the way. The truth is, Mrs. Tafa doesn't want her touching the dough for fear she'll spread her parents' disease.

Mama and I have one last look at Sara. We rest her favorite toy beside her, a striped sock puppet with wobbly button eyes. Then Mama holds me and Mr. Bateman nails down the lid.

The coffin slides into its trailer. Mama, Jonah, and I take our places in the Chevy and the funeral procession heads to the cemetery.

12

THE CEMETERY IS A ROCKY FIELD on the outskirts of town. It only opened last year but already it's almost full. Sara's being buried in the northeast corner, about a ten-minute walk from Esther's parents.

We drive through a gate in the barbed-wire fence, past a metal sign announcing township bylaws for behavior: no screaming, shouting, or other indecent behavior; no defacing or stealing memorials; no grazing of livestock.

The winding dirt roads are filled with potholes. Last rainy season, hearses got stuck in them. So did the tow trucks that came to pull them out. Today, as the Chevy bounces along, I'm more afraid the bouncing may break Sara's coffin.

We pull up to the site. We're not alone. There's a row of eight fresh graves, the earth piled high at the head of each hole. Mr. Bateman says we're the third one down. Funerals are already in progress on either side. In the distance I see the dust of other processions driving through the gates. Mourners hop off pickup trucks and search for their dead. A fight breaks out over who's supposed to be in holes five and six.

Meanwhile, our priest climbs to the top of Sara's mound and delivers a scripture reading about eternal life. I want to believe in God and Sara being with the ancestors. But suddenly I'm scared it's just something priests make up to take away the nightmares. (I'm sorry God, forgive me. I'm sorry God, forgive me. I'm sorry God, forgive me.)

The priest starts the Lord's prayer. "Raetsho yoo ko le godimong." Everyone bows their heads except for me. As we join the priest in chanting the prayer, I stare at this field covered with bricks. Each brick marks a grave. A date's scrawled in black paint. There's not even room for a name. The dead have disappeared as if they never lived.

This is what Sara will have.

"Sara," I whisper, "forgive us." I know we can never afford to buy her a headstone, but I want to save for a moriti; I want her to have a grave marked with its own little fence and canvas top, her name soldered in wire at the front. I want there to be a gate and a lock, too, so I can leave toys for her without them disappearing.

Mama says moritis are just another way to make the undertakers rich. Papa's and my brothers' lost their canvas tops years ago, and the fences bent out of shape the moment the graves collapsed in the rainy season. But I don't care.

On the cattle posts, my great-great-grandparents' graves are marked by river rocks. It doesn't matter, though, because families are together, and everyone knows where everyone's buried going back to forever. But here the dead are buried so helterskelter they get forgotten. Their memory vanishes like tufts of milkpod on the wind.

The priest finishes his prayer and makes the sign of the cross. Mr. Bateman's men lower Sara's coffin on ropes. One by one we file up and throw in our flowers. Then everyone but Mama, me, Jonah, and his brothers-in-law drifts back to our place for the burial feast.

Jonah's brothers-in-law fill the grave with dirt. When they're done, Jonah collapses across the mound. He wails like a baby. Mama strokes his hair. I hate him. He got drunk while Sara was sick. If he didn't care then, why does he pretend to care now? And why does Mama comfort him?

I look at the clouds until Jonah steadies himself. He gets up and wipes his eyes on his tie. Mama brushes the dirt from his jacket and pants, and we head home to join the rest of the mourners.

By the time we arrive, the yard is full, everyone talking to each other over goat stew and cornbread. Mr. Bateman has passed out programs. The cover has a photo of Sara in her coffin and a Bible verse: "Suffer the little children to come unto me, and forbid them not, for of such is the Kingdom of Heaven."

The priest calls the gathering to order. He gives a short speech and turns to Mama, who thanks everyone for coming. After that there's a million hymns led by Mrs. Tafa, who thinks she has a calling for the stage. The yard is alive with singing and clapping. We're hugged, and held, and rocked. Then things blur, and before it seems possible our visitors are gone, except for Esther who's helping to clean up, and Mr. Bateman who's clearing away his tent.

Everyone's moved on. Everyone but Sara. She's frozen in time. Alone in the ground. One and a half forever.

13

BY MIDAFTERNOON IT'S TOO HOT TO BREATHE. The day should be over but it isn't. And Mama and I should be under a tree but we aren't. We're waiting by the roadside with Auntie Lizbet for the pickup to take her back to Tiro. Mama and Auntie Lizbet have big straw hats and are sitting on kitchen chairs that were left outside. I'm cross-legged on the ground shading my head with an old piece of newspaper.

Some people say, "Misery loves company"; I say, sometimes company *is* misery. Instead of talking, we fan ourselves with paper plates from the burial feast and listen to the piercing drone of the cicadas. Each second takes forever. We stifle yawns. The silence is heavier than the heat.

Every so often Auntie Lizbet sighs and taps her foot: "No sense you folks waiting out here on my account."

"No, no, we're happy to," Mama replies quickly. I wish she wasn't so polite.

Just when I think I'm going to yawn so wide my head'll turn inside out, the pickup turns the corner. Mama helps lift Auntie Lizbet onto her feet.

"I'm glad you could make the trip," Mama says.

"I know my duty," Auntie Lizbet replies stiffly. She waits till the driver's hoisted her onto the flatbed and the pickup's started to lurch forward. Then she leans over the open side wall. "It's a terrible price your Sara paid."

"What?" Mama says.

"As you sowed, so you reap, sister. 'The sins are visited upon the children.' Hear the spirits of your ancestors. Repent. Beg forgiveness of those you wronged and dishonored."

The pickup kicks up dust and stones. It disappears around the bend. Mama stands in the road, like someone's kicked her in the guts. She staggers to a stool. I know I should leave her alone but I don't. I run up and kneel beside her.

"Are you all right?"

"I'm fine," she whispers.

"What did Auntie mean?"

"Nothing." She closes her eyes and holds up her hand.

"Please, Mama, open your eyes. Don't make me disappear." Her eyes flash wide, but my voice is a river. Words pour from my heart. "Why does she hate us? Why does our *family* hate us?"

"They don't."

"They do. They didn't come to the funeral. Why? I know the excuses, but *why*? And when Papa died—why did we stay here? Why didn't we go to Tiro?"

"I'm too tired to argue."

"I'm not arguing. I just need to know. Who was dishonored? What was the sin?"

"You ask too many questions."

"I have a right to know."

"I'll tell you when you're older."

"That's what you said when Papa died. Well, I'm older now. Sixteen. When you were sixteen you were married with babies."

Mama looks away. I wrap my arms around her waist. She cradles my head and rocks me. I hold her tight. Finally, when I'm still, she tells me the truth. "They hate us because they say I bring bad luck. They say your papa and I dishonored them."

Her voice may be quiet, but the words are strong and clear—as if the story has rolled around inside her head for so long, it's turned to smooth hard stone.

She says the curse goes back twenty-five years. Her parents—my Granny and Grampa Thela—were good friends with the Malungas, who owned the neighboring cattle post. The families arranged for Mama to marry the Malungas' oldest son, Tuelo.

Tuelo was handsome and strong. It didn't matter. Mama loved Papa. At a harvest celebration, the two of them ran off to Papa's cattle post. My mama-grampa and the Malunga men took up torches and machetes, determined to kill Papa's family and bring Mama home.

There was nearly a bloodbath. But Mr. Malunga found a way to save face. Mama had two younger sisters. Tuelo would get his pick. Also, the bride price would be doubled, but paid by Papa's family in cattle.

Lives were saved; they were also changed. Papa had to restock his family's post. This was hard since Mama came with nothing. So his brothers turned him into a kind of servant. After sixteen years, he'd had enough. He told them he'd repaid his debt, and demanded his share of the harvest. They refused. That's why we came to Bonang.

There were troubles for Mama's family, too.

Her two younger sisters were my aunties Lizbet and Amanthe. Auntie Lizbet was older, so she expected to become Tuelo's wife. This suited her fine, since she was secretly in love with him. But Tuelo chose Auntie Amanthe instead.

Auntie Lizbet blames this on why she never got to marry. (Mama's too kind to say so, but the real reason is Auntie's clubfoot. Building huts, fetching water, and chasing children keeps wives on their feet, especially at cattle posts. The men in Tiro were just being practical. Or maybe they didn't like the idea of being stuck with a toad. Those are hard truths for Auntie Lizbet to swallow. Instead, she blames her life on Mama. Does bad luck make people miserable? Or do miserable people bring bad luck?)

Anyway, right after the wedding, Auntie Amanthe got pregnant. The baby got stuck inside. They had to cut into her belly to get it out. Auntie Amanthe bled to death; the baby was stillborn. At the funeral, Mama was shunned. Auntie Lizbet said what people were thinking: "It should have been you."

After that, whenever anything went wrong Mama got blamed: she'd shamed her parents and dishonored the ancestors. Traditional doctors came to Granny and Grampa Thela's post to take away the evil. But no matter how often they came, Mama's sin was too great. The next time there was a problem, Mama was blamed again.

Mama strokes my hair. "That's why we didn't go back to Tiro. I wouldn't live in a place where people said we got what we deserved."

We sit still for a long time. Then I say: "Granny and Grampa don't really believe in spirit doctors, do they?"

Mama thinks about this for a long time. "There's what people believe," she says, tapping her head. "And there's what they *believe*." She taps her heart. I look down.

Mama lifts my head and cups it in her hands. "Everyone believes in something," she says. "Well, here's what *I* believe. There's no sin in love. What your papa and I did was good. It brought you into the world. And I wouldn't change that for anything."

PART TWO

14

IT'S JUST BEFORE DAYBREAK. I'm sitting on the floor at the foot of Mama's bed. I've been doing this for three months now, ever since the funeral.

Three months. Sara's funeral feels like yesterday and forever all at once. When I come home from school I still expect to see her. In my head, I know she's gone. But in my heart, well, that's something else again.

Everything's changed. Once I knew every pore of Sara's face. Now I don't know anything. I stare at Mr. Bateman's Polaroid of her in her coffin. It doesn't look like her. Or does it? I can't be sure. Why can't I remember? What's wrong with me?

Friends are no help. Whenever I think life's back to normal, one of them will ask, "How are you doing?" and the pain roars back. It's like when I was up north in the delta, learning to pole a mokoro through river reeds; the minute I'd relax I'd hit a patch of roots and capsize.

"People who ask 'how-are-you-doing' aren't friends," says Esther. "They're scab-pickers. Nosy little scab-pickers. What they really want is to know you feel bad so they can feel superior."

"That's not fair."

"It's true."

Nights are the worst. I have horrible dreams. Such as: Sara is dying, but if I get her to the hospital right away she'll be all right. I try to strap her in my bicycle basket, but she keeps falling out, and when I go to pick her up she slides through my hands. Time is disappearing, Sara is dying, it's all my fault.

I wake up in a cold sweat, but being awake is no better. I toss and turn, panicking about time and life and what is the point of anything. Mostly, though, I hurt myself about Sara. Why did I hate her for screaming? Why did I wish she'd stop? Why didn't I rock her more? Did she think I didn't love her? Did she think I didn't care? Is that why she died? Is it my fault? My brain cramps so bad I want to rip off the top of my head. That's when I get up and sit beside Mama.

The first time I did it, the night after the funeral, she was awake too, in her rocking chair. "Go back to bed," she said. "You'll feel better if you get a good night's sleep."

"So why don't you go back to bed?" I asked.

"I'm waiting up for Jonah."

"What makes you think he's coming?"

"Don't talk that way."

"What way?"

"You know what way."

I didn't say another word. I'd guessed right, though. Jonah

didn't show up that night or the night after. In fact, the whole first month after the funeral he only came by three times. Each time he was so drunk I think he stumbled here by accident. Mama never asked where he'd been—I doubt if he could have remembered—she just aimed him for the bedroom.

Sometimes I'd see him when I was out doing errands. He'd be tossing dice on a corner sidewalk or face down in a gutter. I always ignored him. Even if Mama missed him, I was glad we were rid of his stink.

The last time I saw him was different. I'd traded our eggs and vegetables for some milk and sugar at Mister Happy's food stand and was heading back by the rail lands. Along the road there's a chain-link fence with barbed wire on top to keep out trespassers. It doesn't work, though; people just crawl underneath. They sneak into the boxcars on the side rails for sex. Every so often cops clear the place, but an hour later the traffic's back.

At any rate, I was near my turnoff when I saw Jonah, his arm draped over Mary's shoulder, heading to one of the trains. It was one thing seeing them drunk together at the shebeen. But to be shaming Mama out in public—No!

I scrambled under the fence. "Hold it right there!"

When they saw me coming, they tried to hide their heads and change direction. Only they didn't know where to turn. Their legs got tangled. They collapsed in a heap.

I lit into Jonah like a jackal. "Listen, you. If you want to leave my mama, go right ahead. But at least have the guts to tell her first."

"Don't talk to your step-papa like that!" Mary sputtered.

"I'll talk to him any damn way I please," I said. I whirled back on Jonah. "You think you can just walk away. All Mama's questions—her whys—the hurts from not knowing—none of that bothers you, you piece of dung."

"You have your nerve, girl," Jonah quivered.

"I have nerve? You step out with your slut in broad daylight and I have nerve? Papa wouldn't have left Mama—not ever—but if he had, he'd wouldn't have disappeared like she never mattered. That's the difference between him and you. Papa was a man. You're a pig."

"I don't have to listen to this!" he hollered. "I do what I want."

"Hah! You do what your prick wants!" I gave him the finger and strode off, embarrassed to death at what I'd just done.

Like I said, that was the last time I saw him. In fact, it's the last time anyone saw him. He's disappeared for real. Even Mary doesn't know where he is. I think we'd have heard if he'd turned up dead, so I guess he's alive. Maybe he's at his family's cattle post, or hustling booze at some squat out of town. Who knows?

There's rumors, though. A week after he disappeared, Mama and I were in the yard hanging laundry.

"Where's that man of yours been hiding himself?" Mrs. Tafa called over the hedge. Her voice was all honey—sticky for dirt. She's queen of the scab-pickers, that one.

"Oh he's busy at this and that," Mama replied, so calm she didn't even drop a clothes-peg.

"Glad to hear it," said Mrs. Tafa. "I didn't believe the rumors."

What rumors? I wondered. I'm sure Mama wondered too, but she had too much pride to let on. "Oh 'the rumors,'" she laughed. "Rumors, rumors, rumors. Some poor fools have nothing better to do than gossip."

"Why, that's the Lord's truth," Mrs. Tafa agreed, as if Mama wasn't talking about her. Then she made a remark about her kettle boiling and hurried indoors. I was so proud of Mama for putting Mrs. Tafa in her place that I gave her a wink. She pretended not to notice.

"My joints are giving me a hard time today," she said, nursing her elbows. "Could you finish up? I have to lie down. Maybe take some devil's claw root." Her voice was kind of lost. As if, deep down, the truth had finally hit that Jonah wouldn't be back.

Since then, Mama's hardly waited up at all. Some nights she may pace in the main room, or wander through the garden. But mostly, she curls into a ball on her mattress, clutching a pillow. Sometimes she doesn't get up for a day or two. She'll just lie there, eyes shut, rubbing her temples.

The first time I saw her like that was scary. I told her I was going for a doctor, but she grabbed my wrist. "Don't you dare!" Her eyes blazed. "There's nothing the matter with me. It's just a headache." Then she fell back on her mattress.

I'm used to her headaches now. And she's right. They're nothing to be worried about. If I had everything to think about that she does, I'd have them too. So instead of troubling her with doctor talk, I try to stay cheerful and do the chores she can't.

As soon as the rooster crows, I go to the coop, feed the chickens and collect their eggs. Then, while I make the breakfast, I get Iris and Soly dressed, and lay out a few things for lunch. That leaves me an hour to work in the garden before heading to school. If Mama still isn't herself when I get back, I go to the standpipe for water and make supper. Laundry, housework, and cutting firewood I save for the weekend.

Now, when I sit beside Mama at night, she doesn't tell me to go back to bed. She just pretends she doesn't see me.

She pretends about a lot of things. For instance, she pretends everything's normal. She never talks about Sara in front of Iris or Soly. She never mentions Jonah or her headaches either. It's as if she thinks by pretending everything's fine she can fool us into happiness.

Well, she's wrong.

Soly's started to wet the bed. At night he covers his eyes for shame while I wrap him in a rag towel and stick his legs through a plastic bag. Iris has been surprisingly kind, considering it's her bed too. She's only called him a baby once.

She's been mean about other things, though. Soly waits all morning to play with her. But when she gets back from kindergarten, she tricks him. "Let's play hide and seek," she says. Only once he's gone to hide she doesn't bother looking for him. Instead, she sneaks off to explore the neighborhood. Eventually Soly comes out of his hiding place crying. When I get back from school I head out to find her.

It isn't easy. Iris can be anywhere. The playground, the gravel pit, the junkyard at the end of the road...

"Are you crazy, child?" Mama demands when I haul her in. "That junkyard's a menace. Full of old iceboxes and trunks. Little ones like you get themselves locked inside and suffocate to death. As for that gravel pit—you could break your neck."

It's in one ear and out the other. The next day Iris is off again.

Yesterday I caught her at the back of the junkyard behind a pile of bicycle tires, peeking over the lip of the abandoned well. I grabbed her by the arm. "What do you think you're doing?"

"Playing with Sara."

"That's a wicked lie," I said. "Sara isn't anywhere near this junkyard."

"Yes, she is. She lives here."

"Where?"

"Sara says I'm not supposed to tell. It's a secret."

I held her shoulders firmly. "Whoever, or whatever, you've seen at this junkyard, it isn't Sara. Sara's an angel. She doesn't want you getting hurt."

"You don't know what she wants. You and Mama don't even love her anymore. You just want her to go away."

"No we don't."

Iris stuck her fingers in her ears. "Do do do do do do do!" she cried. "Well, if Sara goes away, I'm going away with her."

If I didn't know better, I'd swear Iris was possessed. But I do know better. In English class, Mr. Selalame talks a lot about the supernatural, comparing stories about wizards in Western folk-lore to our tales about traditional doctors. He says there are superstitions all over the world. For instance, in the West, some people use lucky numbers for lotteries. They think a magic number can make them rich.

"People believe in superstitions to make sense of what they can't understand," Mr. Selalame says.

I know he's right. All the same, when Iris mentions her imaginary friend, I chant a prayer to protect against evil spirits. I feel silly, but why take chances? If this is an evil spirit, I'm terrified where it may lead her next. Especially if it decides to come at night.

15

WHEN MAMA'S UP TO IT, which is usually, we spend early Sunday mornings touring "the ring of death." That's what Esther calls the cemeteries circling Bonang.

We leave at dawn in the Tafas' pickup truck. Mrs. Tafa drives while Mr. Tafa stays behind to babysit Iris and Soly. He lets the two of them play in the mud and pretend to help him patch the holes in his tenants' walls. Soly says when he grows up he wants to make houses, like Mr. Tafa. Iris rolls her eyes; she wants to be a foreman and give orders.

Mama feels guilty that Mr. Tafa's stuck with the kids.

"But he loves them," I say. "Besides, he's probably happy to get Mrs. Tafa out of his hair. Even happier that he doesn't have to watch her drive."

"Chanda," Mama laughs, "you shouldn't say things like that."

"Why not?" I laugh back. "It's the truth. If he knew how she tears around in his company truck, he'd have a heart attack."

He would, too. Mrs. Tafa is the scariest driver in the world. She's so busy nibbling treats from the bag on her lap that she hardly ever looks at the road. When she does, it's to stick her head out the window and yell at whoever she almost hit. Meanwhile, we're taking curves so fast I'm surprised we don't fly to the moon.

All the same, I shouldn't complain. Mama and I are lucky our relatives share cemeteries with Mrs. Tafa's, and that she's willing to drive. Otherwise, our trips would be impossible. We can't afford taxis, local buses are rare, and Mama's legs aren't up to biking. (It's times like this I envy the white families who run the diamond mines. They can afford spots in the cemetery downtown, with marble headstones, a gardener to keep things nice, and plots big enough for all their relatives to be together.)

Our first stop is the graveyard where Papa and my brothers are buried, along with Mrs. Tafa's first husband. It's near the mine. For a few years after they died, we came by all the time.

But after a while we started to miss a week here and there, until before I knew it we were only coming on special occasions. I'm glad we're visiting again. Everyone says, "Life goes on," but it's awful to leave the people who loved you, even if you remember them with stories.

Papa and my brothers are buried a piece from the road. In the beginning, Mama took my arm to make it over the rough ground. Now she uses a walking stick she got from Mrs. Tafa. It was left behind by a former tenant. The handle is carved to look like an eagle. Mama thinks it looks so nice she's started to take it everywhere, even to the store. "Be careful," I say. "People will think you're an old lady." She tells me not to be silly.

Anyway, at the graves we say a few prayers. Then I rake the ground until it's tidy, while Mama and Mrs. Tafa share their stories from the mine. Mama's too tired to laugh the way she used to, even at the story of Papa and the black beans. But she manages to smile.

The next cemetery we go to is home to Mr. Dube and of one of Mrs. Tafa's sisters. We pray and tidy there, too. Then we drive to the cemetery where Sara is buried, along with Mrs. Tafa's son Emmanuel. As soon as we pass through the gate, Mrs. Tafa's cheeks go tight. She daubs the crumbs from her mouth, turns right, and hums a memorial song from her village.

We can see Emmanuel's plot from a distance. Mr. Tafa built him a moriti on a base of brick and concrete. Every week Mrs. Tafa unlocks the miniature gate in front and adds another plastic flower wrapped in cellophane. The moriti was getting pretty full until last month when vandals took a machete to the nylon roof and stole them all.

When she saw what had happened, Mrs. Tafa couldn't get

out of the truck. She just sat behind the wheel sobbing, "Why? Why?" The look on her face made me ashamed of all the awful things I've ever thought about her.

Mama held her the way I'd hold Esther. "It's all right, Rose," she comforted. "Emmanuel doesn't mind. He was always so generous. His flowers are with poor souls who didn't have any."

After prayers for Emmanuel, we visit Sara. Her mound has barely settled. The plot number painted on her brick is still fresh. Mama and I can't afford artificial flowers, but if a wild hedge is in bloom, we break a sprig for her. Otherwise we write a poem on a piece of paper and leave it under a stone. It's not much, but it's something.

Once Mama's ready, she and Mrs. Tafa get back in the pickup and I haul my bicycle off the flatbed. While they drive back home to get the others ready for church, I head twenty rows over to be with Esther at her parents' burial site. She's always there waiting for me. Since she doesn't go to school much, it's the one place we're certain to meet. (I could always bike to her place, but she's made me promise not to. She says her auntie and uncle would shame her.)

Mrs. Tafa used to drive me to the Macholos' graves. She and Mama would park at the side of the road while Esther and I said prayers. Only Mrs. Tafa was always rude about the way Esther dressed. "No respect. Not even for her own dead parents," she'd say. "You'd think the little tramp was going to a dance."

One day I finally had enough. When Mama and I got home, I said: "Don't have Mrs. Tafa take me to the Macholos' graves anymore. I'll bring my bike and go on my own."

Mama frowned. "You won't make it back in time for church."

"Being with Esther's more important."

Mama got a troubled look. Then she sat me down beside the washtub. "I know you and Esther are good friends," she said. "You've known each other since we moved to Bonang. All the same, I think maybe you shouldn't see her so often."

My heart thumped into my mouth. "I hardly see her at all."

Mama ignored me. "I like Esther. She's a nice girl. But people have started to say things."

"You mean Mrs. Tafa has started to say things."

"I mean *people*."

I looked at my feet. "What sorts of things?" I asked, as if I didn't know.

"Things about boys."

"Esther flirts, that's all."

Mama paused. "Chanda, folks judge other folks by the company they keep. I don't want you to be Esther's friend anymore. I'd hate for people to say things about *you*."

I was sweating all over. Even the back of my wrists and knees. "Mama," I pleaded, "this isn't you talking, I know it. You don't care about what people say. If you did, you'd never have run off with Papa."

Mama took my hands. "This is different," she said gently. "You're my baby. I worry about you."

"Mama, Esther has no one. If I cut her off, what kind of person would I be?"

Mama had no answer. She took a deep breath and gave me a hug so long and hard I thought she'd never let go. You see, she knew I was right. I can't abandon Esther. She's alone now. Her little brothers and sister are gone.

It's nobody's fault. All the same, Esther blames her aunties and uncles. After the doctor saw her mama, Esther asked them for help. Her papa's oldest brother, her Uncle Kagiso Macholo, spoke for the family. He said they'd send food and whatever they could, but they lived too far away to do much else. The exception was her Auntie and Uncle Poloko, from her mama's people. They lived nearby in a section of Bonang even poorer than ours.

When I first saw the Polokos, it was obvious they hated Esther's whole family. She says it's because they were jealous of her papa's job at the mine. Sickness didn't make them friends. Her uncle chopped a bit of firewood; her auntie fixed some meals. But they were scared of the rubber gloves, so they never came inside. Instead, they'd sit in the yard and pray.

Esther did everything else until the funeral. Then the out-of-town relatives arrived. After the burial feast, they had a meeting in the main room to see who'd look after Esther and her brothers and sister. It went on for hours.

I waited outside with Esther until her Uncle Kagiso called her to join the circle. As soon as the front door closed, I sat under the window and listened through the shutters. Esther's aunties and uncles tried to be kind, but the truth was hard. "None of us can afford to take you all," her Uncle Kagiso said. "We can barely feed our own. But there's an auntie and uncle for each of you."

"No," Esther said. "We have to stay together. We're a family."

"We're *all* of us family," her Uncle Kagiso replied.

"I know, Uncle. But my brothers and sister and me, we need each other. If nobody can take us all, I'll look after things by myself."

"How? The mine is taking back the house, the sickness and funerals have eaten your savings, and there's nothing to sell except some old dishes and furniture. Where will you live? How will you eat? Where will you get the money for clothes, shoes, medicine, school...?"

Esther didn't have an answer. There wasn't one. And so her family was broken up.

One brother went to her Uncle Kagiso, the other to an uncle who was looking for herd boys. Her little sister went to an auntie with cataracts who needed help with sewing. The family knew that Esther's parents wanted her to finish school. Since the best one was in Bonang, and since she'd have a better chance to get married into families that already knew her, Esther was placed with her Auntie and Uncle Poloko. You could tell they didn't want her, but they couldn't say no.

That night I stayed with Esther as her brothers and sister were taken away. They clung to her. They wouldn't stop screaming. Her aunties and uncles had to pry them loose. If Soly or Iris were taken away like that, I'd die.

I get just as upset thinking about Esther's life with the Polokos. She's supposed to go to school, but according to her, they keep her like a servant. After cooking and cleaning and yard work, she has to babysit her nieces and nephews. There're six of them under ten. They hit her and scratch her and call her names, and if she does anything to stop them, they scream that she's hurting them, and her auntie hits her with a fry pan.

If she complains, her uncle gets mad. "You think you're a big shot like your mama and papa, with their running water and their flush toilet!" he yells. "Well, you're no more special than us. While you live under our roof, you do what we say."

Whenever she can, Esther sneaks off. It's trickier on weekdays. Her uncle fixes shoes part-time on the pavement outside

Quality Fashions, and her auntie does shift work at KFC. She has to wait till they're both gone, and hope the monsters don't tell on her.

Sundays, escape is easier. The entire family goes to church at Bethel Gospel Hall. In the beginning, they made Esther come along too, but she wouldn't sing the hymns or pray. So now, for the sins of pride and blasphemy, they make her stay home and scrub the outhouse. Of course, she never does. Instead, she takes off to the cemetery to be with her mama and papa. And me.

Luckily, we get to visit for a long time, on account of Bethel Gospel has the longest services in town. From early morning to late afternoon everyone's singing, dancing, and speaking in tongues. Sometimes they fall down, "slain in the Lord."

Once when her mama was sick, Esther got a performance in her own front yard. The Polokos brought over their congregation for an exorcism. I was helping with her mama when they danced up the road swishing their robes and thumping their tambourines. It was like a parade and a circus all at once.

The priest made a hullabaloo about sin and disease. "It's Satan has brought sickness to this house!" He blessed a tin cup of holy water and mopane ash, and said the fiend would be cast out and Mrs. Macholo would be saved if she'd come to the door and drink it. Esther said her mama couldn't move, much less come to the door; she was on her deathbed.

"That's the devil talking," said the priest. "With God, all things are possible." No sooner had the words left his lips than he was seized by the Spirit. He pushed his way inside and tried to force the holy water down Mrs. Macholo's throat. Esther felt dirty. I can't imagine how her mama felt. It was like the priest was blaming her for dying.

It's because of that that Esther doesn't pray or sing hymns anymore. Once she stood on her mama's grave and shouted: "If God could save Mama and Papa and didn't, I hate Him. And if He *couldn't* save them, He's useless. Priests and church ladies should go straight to hell."

"Don't say that! Don't even think it!" I said. "Not all churches are like your auntie and uncle's. Our priest talks about joy and peace and everlasting love."

"Blah blah blah." Esther made a face. "God-talk is just superstitious mumbo jumbo."

"That's not true."

"It is so. Priests are no better than spirit doctors. The only difference is that you believe in one and not the other."

I wish Esther wouldn't be like that, but I try not to judge her. I don't think God judges her either, not after what she's gone through. She doesn't have a home, a family, or anything to believe in anymore. No wonder she likes to get her picture taken at the Liberty. It's the one way she gets to feel important.

16

AS USUAL, THIS SUNDAY ESTHER'S ALREADY WAITING for me when I roll up. She's lying on her mama's grave daydreaming, in those lime capri pants she picked up at the bazaar. They're filthy and torn. But that's not what I notice first. It's her right eye, all purple and swollen shut.

I hop off my bike. "What happened?"

Esther looks up with a lopsided grin. "Last night Auntie threw the iron at my head."

"Why?"

She roars with laughter. "She told me to do the laundry. I told her to shove it up her ass."

"That's not funny. You've been beaten before. Next time call the cops."

"Don't be stupid." Esther stretches. "Auntie'd say I was lying and I'd get another whupping from my uncle. Either that or they'd kick me onto the street. Then what would I do?"

"You could live with us."

Esther groans. "Your mama doesn't want me around."

"That's not true," I lie.

"It is so. Anyway, I don't want to talk about it." She cartwheels in my direction.

I leap out of her way. "You're worse than Soly and Iris put together!"

"I hope so," she winks. Or tries to wink.

We walk to our favorite spot, an uprooted tree stump by a bend in the road. As we go, we collect flat, smooth stones. Once we've arrived, we hunch on the stump and take turns tossing them at the pothole on the far side of the bend. It's a game we started weeks ago. In the beginning, we thought we'd have it filled by rainy season, but at the rate we're going I wouldn't count on it.

I tell Esther about yesterday, and how Iris claims she's playing with Sara.

"If you want my opinion," Esther says, "you should bring her to Sara's grave." She lands a stone perfectly. "I mean it. Seeing where Sara's buried would make it real for her. Then maybe this imaginary friend would go away." She lands a second.

"Mama says she's not old enough."

"According to adults we're never old enough. For anything." She lands her third in a row. "If it weren't for me, my brothers and sister would still be asking when they're coming home."

Esther's forehead wrinkles up. She's with me in body, but her mind is far away. We sit like this for awhile, Esther thinking and me watching her think. At last I say: "Any news from your brothers?"

Esther shakes her head. "It's not like the cattle posts have phones." She looks away. "Anyway, maybe not hearing from them is better. I hate when blind Auntie travels to town with my little sister. When they go to leave, my sister hangs off my neck crying, 'Keep me with you!' I tell her I can't, but she doesn't understand." Esther gets up and pitches a stone as far as she can. "Well, things are going to change. I have a plan. This time next year we'll all be together."

"How?"

"It's a secret."

"Tell me." But before I can get her to explain, she's let out a hoot and begun to run back to her parents' gravesite. "Race you to the bikes!"

"No fair," I yell. "You have a head start."

We say a good-bye to her parents and begin the long ride home. At the crossroads leading to Esther's section, we stop for a final chat, rocking on our bike seats, touching the ground on tiptoes. We're talking about nothing in particular, when Esther says: "I'm sorry your mama's not feeling well."

"Who says she isn't?"

"Nobody," Esther says carefully. "I just see her using a cane."

"It's not a cane. It's a walking stick."

"Whatever you call it, she uses it all the time."

"So what? She doesn't want to sprain her ankle. It's pretty rocky around here. Besides, she likes it."

Esther takes a long pause. "I'm only going to ask this once," she says, "and please don't take it the wrong way, but you're my best friend, and I really love you, and I don't want anything bad to happen to you, and—"

"And and and. What are you trying to say?"

Esther looks down. She twists the rings on her fingers. "Does your mama have a will?"

For a second I can't breathe.

"Well, does she?"

"Why would you ask something like that?"

"No reason."

"There's nothing the matter with Mama." My palms sweat against the handlebar grips.

"All right, I believe you," Esther presses. "It's just—if there was an accident or something, who'd get the house? Who'd get the garden?"

"Stop it. Talking about death and wills is bad luck."

"That's what Mama and Papa used to say."

"What do they have to do with *my* mama?" I wipe my hands on my skirt.

"Nothing," she says. "It's only, at Sara's funeral I remember your Auntie Lizbet. I hope the rest of your relatives are nicer."

"Shut up, Esther. I hate you." I punch her hard. She topples over onto the ground.

I can't believe what I've done. "I'm sorry," I blubber. I help her up. Her hands are scraped. I'm certain she'll want to fight, but she doesn't. She checks her elbows. There's a trickle of blood. I pull out a tissue but she won't take it. She gets back on her bike and rides off without saying anything.

"Esther, don't go!" I shout. I cycle hard to catch up with her.

"Don't go till you tell me everything's okay between us."

She slams on her brakes. Her bike skids on the gravel to a sideways stop. "Fine," she says. "Everything's '*okay*,' Chanda. Everything's perfect. Happy? Now leave me alone."

17

I HATE HAVING FIGHTS WITH ESTHER. When she decides to get mad, she can stay mad forever. And she hates to apologize for anything—even when a fight is partly her fault.

In the old days we never used to fight. At least not about anything important. It was always over little things. Such as, once before high school I told her she should spend less time on her looks and more time on her books. She made a face and told me if I didn't stop reading I'd go blind.

"Good. Then I wouldn't have to look at your stupid clothes," I shot back. "All those big clunky heels and halter tops. The least you could do is cover your navel. You're going to get a reputation."

"All the better to get kissed," she squealed.

I said she was a flirt, she said I was a nun, and that was about it.

Since high school the fights have gotten real. A few months after Sara was born there was a dance. Esther ran up the next day all excited and told me what she'd done with her date in the bushes behind the soccer field. I was half-horrified, half-curious: "I hope you're making that up."

"Why would I make it up?" she said. "There's nothing wrong with a little fooling around. Just because Isaac Pheto was a pervert doesn't mean you have to hate men."

I went crazy. I called her names, wrestled her to the ground, and ripped the combs out of her hair. "I should never have told you about that!" I cried.

"I'm sorry," she said. "I'm sorry, I'm sorry, I didn't mean it." It's the one time she's ever apologized right away.

"It's not like you're right, either," I said, when things had settled down. "What Isaac did gives me nightmares. But I loved Papa more than anything, not to mention Mr. Dube and my older brothers. Then there's Soly, Mr. Tafa, Joseph and Pako from math class—and Mr. Selalame, of course. I like lots of men."

Esther paused. "So why don't you ever go out?"

"I'm busy. Haven't you noticed? My new sister's got colic, and Mama needs help. Iris and Soly are no use, Jonah never lifts a finger, so that leaves me to do everything."

It's been two years since I said that, and I'm still stuck. I try not to think about it, but sometimes I get mad at Mama for being tired and leaving me to take care of everything. Then I feel guilty for being selfish. Then I get mad for feeling guilty. What's the matter with me?

Anyway, it was easy to patch things up when Esther came to school. Seeing each other all day, I'd know when it was safe to start talking again. Now I have to guess. But what if I guess wrong? I've promised never to go to her auntie and uncle's. So if she's still angry and I bike over, she'll bite my head off. Or if I stake out the Liberty, she'll accuse me of spying.

That means I'm left waiting for *her*, wondering if she's forgiven me yet. The not-knowing makes me anxious. Which makes me upset. Which makes me mad at her all over again.

Right now I'm *really* mad. It's been almost a week since I shoved her off her bike. I didn't expect to see her on Monday or Tuesday, and I understood her staying away on Wednesday and Thursday. Even on Friday. But now it's Saturday morning. Is she really angry or just punishing me? Either way, it isn't fair. I shouldn't have pushed her, but she shouldn't have talked about Mama as if she was dying either.

I think about this as I plant bean rows in the garden. Who does Esther think she is, anyway? A doctor? Since when does using a walking stick mean you're sick? Honest to god, Esther makes me so mad I wish she was here just so I could tell her to go away.

I drop bean seeds into the new holes and count my blessings. Mama got one of her headaches on Thursday and she's still in bed. The last thing I need is for Esther to know *that*. If she can see death in a cane, think what she could imagine in a headache. Aren't there enough real problems in the world without people like Esther imagining pretend ones?

Maybe Mama is right. Maybe I shouldn't be her friend. I jab my spade into the ground over and over and over. ABCDEFG, ABCDEFG, ABCDEFG.

"Chanda!"

I've stabbed my spade beside Mrs. Tafa's foot. I look up. She balloons over me; her dress is like a floral parachute with legs.

"You're quite the whirlwind," she says. I freeze. Whenever Mrs. Tafa gives a compliment, it pays to be suspicious. "The speed you dig, no wonder your mama doesn't need to garden anymore."

"Thank you, Auntie," I say. "But Mama works twice as hard as me." I pretend to get back to work.

Mrs. Tafa doesn't take the hint. After staring at me for a quarter row, she says: "She's having another sleeping day, isn't she?"

"No," I lie. "As a matter of fact, she's inside sewing."

"Well, if she's up, I'll pop in to say hello." Mrs. Tafa heads toward the front door.

I get in her way. "Auntie, I don't mean to be unkind, but Mama doesn't want visitors today."

Once upon a time, Mrs. Tafa would have patted me on the head and brushed me aside, but I'm bigger now. She steps back. "Nothing serious, I hope."

"Just a headache."

Mrs. Tafa taps her nose slowly. "A word to the wise," she whispers. "These headaches have got to stop."

"She doesn't get them on purpose. They're on account of her grieving."

"Grieving or not, people talk."

A sliver of ice shoots up my spine. "No one has the right to gossip about Mama."

"Folks say what they say, whether they have a right or not." Mrs. Tafa lowers her voice. "Enough silly games, girl. I know who can cure your mama's headaches. Now let me in."

My insides are churning. Mama needs her rest, but if Mrs. Tafa knows someone who can make her pains go away, well... I let her pass. She marches through the door and straight into Mama's bedroom. Mama is curled under a blanket, her head covered by a pillow.

"There's no use pretending you're asleep," Mrs. Tafa barks. She sits on the edge of the bed. "When the accident killed my Emmanuel, I took to bed just like you. What saved me was a cure better than devil's claw root. I got it from a doctor the other side of Kawkee. Far enough away, no one ever knew I needed help."

Mama rolls slowly onto her back. She listens hard.

"His name is Dr. Chilume," Mrs. Tafa continues. "He's smart as a whip. When I first walked into his office, he showed me his medical degrees. He has six of them, all framed, with gold seals, red ribbons, and the fanciest lettering you could imagine. Tomorrow, instead of touring the cemeteries, we'll pay him a visit."

Mama's too tired to talk, but there's a glimmer in her eyes. She nods.

Mrs. Tafa strokes her shoulder. "Don't you worry, Lilian. Dr. Chilume will have you clicking your heels in no time. He's a miracle worker."

18

THE VILLAGE OF KAWKEE is an hour's drive from Bonang. Forty minutes, if you're Mrs. Tafa. I asked Mama if she was up for the trip. "Yes," she said, "yesterday's lie-down did me a world of good." All the same, she's brought along a plastic bag in case of travel sickness.

I'm glad she's seeing a doctor, but as we get in Mrs. Tafa's truck, I wish we were going to the cemetery first. I'd have had the chance to clear things up with Esther. I picture her waiting for me and worrying about why I haven't come. Part of me feels guilty for making her dangle. The other part of me thinks it serves her right for staying away all week.

Mrs. Tafa guns the pickup and suddenly I have other things on my mind. Such as—did I say I wished we were going to the cemetery? The way Mrs. Tafa drives we may end up there after all. Only permanently. She veers around oxcarts at full tilt, even when we're going up hills. She only slows down once—when the road takes a ninety-degree turn and I yell, "Look out! A tree!" Then she jams on the brakes and I grab Mama to keep her from pitching through the windshield.

It doesn't get any better when we leave the paved highway at the Kawkee turnoff. The dirt road is so bumpy our heads nearly bounce through the roof. Worse, it narrows to a single lane. Mrs. Tafa doesn't care. In fact, she hits the accelerator. I scream as children on bicycles head for the ditch to avoid being run down. Mrs. Tafa just laughs and stuffs her face with banana chips.

Mama closes her eyes and holds her stomach.

"Dr. Chilume's the younger brother of the local chief," Mrs. Tafa blabs between mouthfuls. "You ever hear of Chilume Greens?"

"Of course," I say. Does she think I'm stupid? Everybody knows Chilume Greens. It's the company that grows morogo for the supermarket chains.

"Well," Mrs. Tafa winks, "it's Dr. Chilume's family that owns it. He started out running his brothers' farms. Only he was so smart the family sent him to Jo'burg to study herbal medicine. That's where he got his degrees. Cancer, colitis, TB—there's nothing he can't fix. He's even cured folks of *that other thing*."

My jaw drops. "You mean AIDS?"

At the sound of the word, Mrs. Tafa chokes on her banana chips. "That's what I said," she recovers. "He has a secret tonic."

Can that possibly be true? I know there are herbal remedies that work: cinnamon cloves take away toothache pain, mint tea works for constipation, garlic is good for colds, and devil's claw root works for skin and arthritis. But a cure for AIDS? If Mrs. Tafa's right, Dr. Chilume *is* a genius. I think of Esther's parents. I imagine them alive.

We reach the schoolhouse on the edge of Kawkee. Mrs. Tafa

tosses her empty chip bag out the window and turns left. We drive through a forest of jackalberry bushes and mopane trees. It opens up on a dam rimmed by concrete pilings and reed beds. Clusters of men sit on the pilings, or stand waist-deep in the water, fishing. On the other side of the dam, lush green fields dotted with low-lying whitewashed barns spread out to the horizon.

I'm amazed that crops are growing in the dry season. Then I see the haze of rainbows sparkling everywhere. An enormous sprinkler system's been connected to the dam.

Mrs. Tafa makes a wide sweep with her hand. "All those fields belong to the Chilumes. They manage the water for the town. That's the doctor's place." She points across the dam to a modern two-story, stucco house with a tiled roof. "You don't get rich by being stupid," she says.

"I thought we'd be going to a hospital or neighborhood clinic," I say.

"Dr. Chilume's much too good for that," Mrs. Tafa sniffs.

We drive to where the dam narrows. There's a wooden bridge with no railing. The water's low. Despite the algae, I can make out shapes on the silt bottom. The biggest is a van that went over the edge. Its antenna breaks the surface, glistening in the sun.

"Maybe we should walk from here," I say.

Mrs. Tafa takes that as a challenge. She revs the engine. Mama and I hold on for dear life as we clatter across. The rattling boards disturb flocks of birds nesting in the supports. They fly up from everywhere. Meanwhile, the men along the shore shake their fists at us, angry that we've scared away the fish. Mrs. Tafa finds their shaking fists funny. She rolls down the window and waves at them, whooping and honking her horn. I cringe under the dashboard.

Safely on the other side, we ride to a gravel parking lot near the farmhouse, pulling up beside a tractor, three flatbed trucks marked Chilume Greens, and a Toyota Corolla.

Before getting out of the pickup, Mrs. Tafa puts on some lipstick, checking herself in the rearview mirror. "You'll want to give your hair a brush, Lilian," she says to Mama. "And as for you," she turns to me, "there's a patch of dirt on your cheek so big I'd swear you rolled in mud all the way from Bonang."

I wipe the smudge, but that's not good enough for Mrs. Tafa. She whisks her hankie out of her sleeve, spits on it, and daubs my face. No one's done that to me since I was a baby; it nearly makes me sick.

"Don't make such a fuss," Mrs. Tafa says. "I'm your auntie, after all."

A couple of dogs come running toward us. They're called off by a large bald man in an open-necked white shirt, workboots, and jeans. He's got big ears and even bigger hands.

"Dr. Chilume!" Mrs. Tafa calls out.

"Rose. What a surprise," the doctor calls back. He strides up, hitching his jeans up under his belly. "You came in the back way."

"I wanted to show off your dam to my friends."

"You mean the Kawkee dam," he grins. "What can I do for you?"

"I could do with a refill of cystosis tablets," she says. "But the real reason I'm here is on account of my friend." Mrs. Tafa introduces us, explaining how Mama's been feeling poorly on account of Sara's death.

"It's a terrible thing, the loss of a child," Dr. Chilume nods. "All the same, sister, life is for the living. Let's see what we can do."

He leads us to a shed near the farmhouse. It's made of cement blocks with a corrugated tin roof, like something our neighbors might live in, except it has a window with glass panes. "HERBAL CLINIC" is painted in capital letters on the side wall. Underneath, I read the words "Specializing in cures for..." followed by a long list of diseases. Like Mrs. Tafa said, the list includes HIV/AIDS.

My forehead tingles. I point at the sign. "How many AIDS patients do you have?"

Mrs. Tafa gasps as if I'm being rude, but Dr. Chilume just leans against the door frame and smiles. "Too many to count," he says.

"How many do you cure?"

"All of them." He scrapes the mud off his boots. "At least all of the ones who come to me in time. Some folks hold back on account of the cost. They see me when it's too late. My remedy's expensive, but if it's taken early enough, it's guaranteed to work."

"What's it made of?"

"Sorry. I can't say a word until I get my patent."

"Don't mind Chanda's questions," Mama apologizes. "She always wants to know everything about everything."

"Good for her," Dr. Chilume laughs. He ushers us into his shed.

Despite the window, the light inside is dim and there's not much space. A desk, a filing cabinet, and two chrome chairs with plastic-covered cushions take up half the room. The other half is filled by a couple of card tables and a wall of wooden shelves. The shelves are crammed with half-empty pill bottles and battered boxes of bandages, hypodermic needles, and cotton balls. The card tables are a clutter of stuffed brown paper bags, each with the name of a herb written on it in felt marker. Under the tables are stacks of dusty pamphlets, beer cases, and a bathroom scales.

Mama and Mrs. Tafa sit on the chairs as Dr. Chilume puts on the lab coat lying across his desk. He starts his examination by asking Mama her particulars, and having her stand on the scales. Then he opens a desk drawer and fishes a stethoscope from a tangle of catheters. After checking Mama's pulse, he looks up her ears and nose with a flashlight.

Meanwhile, my eyes have gotten used to being out of the sun's glare. I look at all the things hanging on the walls. There's a poster of the human body, like the one on the bulletin board in science class. There's an out-of-date calendar with a photograph of Vic Falls. Lastly, there's the six medical degrees that Mrs. Tafa talked about.

Even from across the room they look impressive in their black metal frames. It's too bad the protective glass is covered in grime; it makes them hard to read. But nothing can disguise the elegance of the lettering and the richness of the decoration. Each of the documents is covered in sweeping squiggles and swirls and there are gold seals and red ribbons, just like Mrs. Tafa said. As Dr. Chilume takes Mama's blood pressure, I wander over for a closer look.

At first, I imagine the words must be in Latin because the lettering's so fancy. But as I stare through the dirt I realize they're in English. The one on the left says: "This is to certify that Mr. Charles Chilume attended the fourth annual Herbatex Company showcase at the Holiday Inn Conference Centre, Johannesburg, South Africa, August 8–10, 1995." It's signed by a "Mr. Peter Ashbridge, Head Herbatex Sales Rep, S.A."

Heart pounding, I examine the other "degrees." All of them say: "This is to certify that Mr. Charles Chilume is a licensed and authorized dealer of Herbatex Company products." Even worse, I realize they've been run off on a photocopier. The gold seals in the corners are just shiny stickers. And the red ribbons are only that: red ribbons, cut with a scissors and stuck to the paper by the stickers.

"Doctor" Chilume went to Jo'burg for medical training, did he? Hah! He went to a pill convention. He's no doctor. He's a salesman. A liar! Trading on fears of disease and death. Preying on folks like Mrs. Tafa who can't read.

"I diagnose insomnia, depression, and a swelling of the joints," he tells Mama. "But don't you worry. I have the remedies. You'll be feeling better in no time."

I swing around prepared to expose him, but I can't. For the first time in ages, Mama's eyes are full of hope.

"To soothe the agitation of the nervous system, I prescribe *Lactuca virosa* and *Passiflora*," Mr. Chilume continues. "They come in tablets to be taken twice a day. For the joints, I prescribe a morning tablet of poke root, bogbean, and celery seed. Finally, to cleanse impurities from the bowel, I prescribe a purgative pill of buckthorn, elder, and senna leaves."

"How much will all that cost?" Mama asks.

"Thirty American dollars to start."

Mama lowers her eyes. "I can't afford it."

"You can't afford not to afford it," Mrs. Tafa whispers, giving her an elbow in the ribs.

I get an idea. "Doctor Chilume," I interrupt, pointing at his Herbatex souvenirs, "are these your medical degrees?"

Mr. Chilume's eyes twitch. "Yes."

"They're very impressive," I smile sweetly. "By the way, do you get your pills from Herbatex?"

Mr. Chilume chokes. "Yes, Herbatex tablets. Imported from Switzerland. The best herbal medicinal tablets money can buy."

"I'm sure they are," I say. "But with all your qualifications, couldn't you mix Mama a treatment from the herbs on your table?"

Mr. Chilume clears his throat. "Herbatex tablets have a secret coating to let them dissolve in the intestinal tract. Nonetheless," he adds quickly, "I can prepare an alternative."

"Just as effective?"

"Of course."

"And affordable?"

"Absolutely." He turns to Mama. "Your daughter's loyalty touches me deeply. So deeply I've decided to give you a free month's treatment."

"Seeing as I'm such a loyal customer," Mrs. Tafa interrupts, "maybe you could give me a discount on my cystosis tablets, too."

"Just this once," Mr. Chilume says grimly. "But don't let it get around or I'll be out of business." He pulls a handful of plastic sandwich bags from his filing cabinet and asks us to step outside while he mixes the herbs. As we leave the shed, I take care to block Mama's view of his official documents. Unlike Mrs. Tafa, she can read, too.

Outside, Mrs. Tafa waddles around in circles. Sitting on the low chrome chair has bunched her underwear up her bum cheeks. "How do you know about Herbatex?" she demands, struggling to wriggle them back into place.

"From school," I lie. "I was in the library researching a science project on herbal remedies. Herbatex was mentioned in a *Reader's Digest* article."

"Is that so? Well, all the same, you have some nerve," Mrs.

Tafa scolds as she twists and turns. "Interrupting a medical consultation to ask a doctor about his supplier. I hate to be unkind, Lilian, but is that how you taught her manners?"

"Hush up," Mama says. "I think Chanda did well for herself."

"Do you now?" Mrs. Tafa gives up trying to be dignified. She braces herself against a nearby tree, reaches up under her dress and gives her underwear a good hard yank.

Mama bursts out laughing. It's a huge laugh, the laugh she had when she was well. Mrs. Tafa and I look at her in amazement. Then we start laughing too. The air dances!

19

WE'RE ALL IN A GOOD MOOD as we arrive home. Iris and Soly run up to the truck to greet us. Mama gives them a hug, then goes over to Mrs. Tafa's for some tea. She holds her herb bags tight to her stomach.

The minute she's gone, Iris pulls a scrap of paper from her pocket. "This is for you. It's from Esther. She just left."

I grab the note.

"Soly ripped the paper from one of your binders. I told him not to, but he did anyway." She smiles brightly. "Are you going to spank him?"

"No," Soly pleads. "It was Iris's idea."

"Don't worry," I say.

Esther's note is written on the back of an old sheet of math homework: "Chanda, Where were you? I waited at the cemetery. I'll bike over later this week. Have to race now, scrub outhouse. Don't want another beating. Esther"

I frown.

"What's wrong?" Soly asks.

"Nothing," I say. "Everything's fine." Everything's fine. I'm starting to sound like Mama. I tell them they're free to play, we won't be going to church today.

"Can I put on my Sunday School dress anyway?" Iris asks.

"No. You'll just get it dirty."

She puts her hands on her hips. "No, I won't. Besides, I have to wear it now. In a few months it'll be too small for me."

Iris makes me laugh. "All right," I say. "But only for ten minutes. And stay inside. If Mama knows I said yes, she'll kill me."

Iris runs indoors happy as a bird. I re-read Esther's note, her fear of "another beating." I remember her black eye last week. If I hurry, maybe I can get to her before her auntie, uncle, and the brats get back from Bethel Gospel Hall. We have to talk. We have to do something. I don't know what, but the beatings have got to stop.

It's a ten-minute hard bike to Esther's. As I whiz along, I hear swearing rippling over the walls of shebeens, and tambourines and singing from inside cement block churches. Twice I stop and bow my head as funeral processions pass. I spot grannies and grampas hunching under trees with their clay pipes, and front yards with Mamas washing children in tin tubs.

How I hated sharing bathwater at the cattle post! As the littlest, I had to wait till my older sister and brothers were done. By the time the water got to me, it was always dirty gray, and the tub was rimmed with soap scum. I remember being happy once because my bath was warm. I stopped being happy when I saw the smirk on my brother's face, who'd just gotten out. But now's not the time for remembering. I've arrived.

If Esther's auntie and uncle were home from church, their kids would be outside playing. But the place is quiet as a tomb. I open the gate and roll my bike over to the shed. This is where they put Esther on account of the house was full.

It's exactly like when I last saw it, the day she moved in. The tin roof's covered in broken barrels and sections of rusty pipe. Esther says the weight of the junk is all that keeps the roof from blowing off. I believe her. A few shovels, a rake, and a hoe are propped against the walls. An overturned wheelbarrow rests on one side of the door beside a couple of buckets.

I tap at the door. "Esther?"

I get an answer. But not from Esther. Instead, there's a huge barking from the scrap pile behind the house. I look up. Her uncle's dogs are tearing around the corner. They charge straight at me. I scramble for a shovel. I trip. Before I can get up, the dogs are all over me. I cover my head with my hands. I bunch up tight.

But they're not biting. They're sniffing. They want to see if I have food. I pat their heads. They wag their tails. I get up.

Esther should have come at the sound of the barking, but no. So where is she? I go to the house and peek through the window slats. "Esther?" Again no answer. I head around back to the outhouse. From twenty feet away I almost throw up. No wonder Esther's auntie told her to clean it. No wonder she didn't.

I re-read Esther's note. She said she had to go home or she'd be beaten. But if she's not in the shed, the house, or the out-house—where is she? And where's her bike? I get a sick feeling in my stomach. Did something happen to her between my place and here?

Don't worry, I think. Esther likely put her bike in the shed for safekeeping. She's probably at the standpipe getting water for cleaning. No, wait—if she went to the standpipe, why are the wheelbarrow and buckets by the shed?

I don't have any more time to think. The dogs have been playing around my feet and knees. Now there's a sound at the front gate; they run to check it out. So do I, expecting to see Esther. Instead, I come face to face with her auntie, uncle, and cousins.

Her auntie's in a green robe and headdress, with a white shoulder cape and sash. Her uncle's robe is also green, capped by a bishop's crown of cloth on cardboard. The little ones are in yellow with green trim. They're at the shed staring at my bike. When they see me coming, their eyes narrow.

"Who are you?" her uncle demands.

"Chanda Kabelo," I say. "We met at Mrs. Macholo's laying over? I helped Esther move in?"

"What do you want?" from her auntie. Her arms are crossed.

I try to think of a good lie, but there aren't any. "I'm looking for Esther."

"Then what are you doing here?" her auntie snorts.

"I thought this was where she lives."

"Is it?"

"Isn't it?" I shift my weight.

"Esther shows up now and then," her auntie says coldly.

I want to yell—"You're lying. Esther slaves for you, you beat her"—but that would only get her in trouble, so I stay shut up. There's an awful silence.

"We don't like strangers in the yard," her uncle says at last. "Least of all strangers who circle our house. How do we know you're not a thief?"

"I told you—I'm a friend of Esther's!"

"Like I said," he replies grimly.

My cheeks flush.

"You better go," says her auntie.

"And don't come back," her uncle adds. "Next time we'll send for the police."

"Go ahead," I think. "While they're here, I'll tell them you beat my friend."

Esther's cousins move away from my bike. I lift it up and walk it to the road. Then I get on and turn back. I clear my throat. "Since Esther's not here, do you have any idea where I could find her?"

"Plenty," her auntie adds. "None fit to repeat."

Her uncle takes off his bishop's hat and wipes his forehead. "Try the Liberty Hotel and work your way down from there."

"If you see her, tell her we've had enough," her auntie says. "Either she lives right or she's gone. It's hard to keep our little ones from sin when they live with a whore."

20

I PEDAL HARD TO THE LIBERTY. Esther a whore? It's a lie. An evil lie. She only lets tourists take her picture. Or maybe pictures count as whoring to the holy hypocrites at Bethel Gospel Hall.

All the same ... why did Esther lie about going home? What's the real reason she made me promise not to visit her place?

I think about the Polaroids. I think about the men who take them. Who give her name to their friends. Who write her on the Internet. Esther laughed when I got upset about it. But I'm right. Tourists can take pictures of anyone. They don't need to send e-mails for that.

I think about the rumors. What Mrs. Tafa's said. And Mama.

And the boys at school. The girls too. I've always taken Esther's side. But what if they're right? What if I'm a fool? No, stop it, stop it. If I think like that, what kind of a friend am I?

I wheel around the Liberty's circular drive. No Esther. What a relief. Or maybe not.

I head to the side streets. At night they're alive with whores in short skirts and bright plastic knee-highs who hop into cars at stop signs. By day they're quiet. Clients are shy of the light, so the action moves into the Sir Cecil Rhodes Commemorative Garden. That's what the guidebooks call it. We just call it hooker park.

It's five blocks long, three wide. There's rapes and murders, but it's okay in the afternoon if you stick to the main sidewalk. Hookers hang out on the benches soaking up sun or catching some sleep. If a guy's interested, they go into the bushes. Or if he's a trucker he'll take them to his van. That's what they say at school, anyway.

The park's surrounded by a stone wall. I go in by the iron gate on the south side and ride around the main route—it's a large figure eight—taking a quick peek up the side trails. At the north end, there's a gully and the sidewalk turns into a foot-bridge. I hear noises underneath, but I'm smart enough not to stop. The third time I bike around, a man is scrambling up the embankment in a hurry. Below, a woman is wiping the inside of her legs with a rag.

I start to relax. Three times around and no sign of Esther. I say a prayer of thanks. What was I thinking? I feel so guilty. I heard a nasty lie and all of a sudden I turned into Mrs. Tafa.

I decide to go to the Red Fishtail Mall. I'll drive in front of Mr. Mpho's Electronics, then check the Internet cafe.

That's my plan at least, but I don't get very far. As I leave the park, a limo with tinted windows stops at the side of the road ahead of me. Someone's getting out of the back seat. Someone very familiar.

"Esther!"

"Chanda!"

The limo takes off. Esther stands in front of me holding a plastic grocery bag. Inside the bag, I see her regular clothes. They're bright as usual, but nothing like what she's wearing now. A ribbon of orange vinyl mini-skirt and a pink lace bikini top. Her face is covered in cheap makeup. The lipstick is smudged.

"What are you doing here?" I say, as if it isn't obvious.

"None of your business," she snaps. "How dare you spy on me?"

"I'm not. I got your note. I went to your place."

"I told you never to go there!"

"I was worried."

"Who cares? You promised you wouldn't. You lied."

"*I* lied?" My eyes pop.

"Anyway, I don't know why you're so upset," she says, more defiant than ever. "It's not like I'm doing anything. I'm giving guided tours, that's all. I take people around the city. Show them places of interest. What's wrong with that?"

"Nothing, if it's the truth. But it's not."

"How do you know? I thought we were friends. Friends are supposed to trust each other."

"Trust!" My eyes fill up. "Do you know how stupid you sound?"

"Me? Stupid?" Esther reaches into her panties and pulls out a roll of paper money. "Does this look stupid? You don't make half this in a month selling your eggs and vegetables. I make it in an afternoon. And you think *I'm* stupid?"

I look from her eyes to the money and back again. The air leaves my body. I totter on my feet. "I believed in you," I whisper. "When people called you names, I always took your side."

Esther's face crumples. "It's easy for you," she says. "You have your mama, your sister, your brother. My mama's dead. My brothers and sister are scattered all over. I want my family. I need the money to get them back."

"By doing *this*?"

"How else can I get enough to support us? To rent a room? Buy food?" She tosses her arms in the air, flops on a nearby bench and turns away.

I lean my bike against a tree and join her. We sit for a long time without saying anything, her wiping her eyes, me staring at the ground.

"How long have you been hooking?" I say at last.

"A few months."

I swallow hard.

"Not every day," she says quickly. As if that reassures me.

"Why didn't you tell me?"

Her voice gets very small. "I didn't think you'd be my friend anymore."

"You know me better than that."

She sniffles. "Who knows anybody?"

Another long pause. "You must have guessed I'd find out."

"Why?" She wipes back a tiny river of mascara. "There's so many rumors about me, I figured you'd just think it was another one. Besides, folks our way don't come here much. If they do, they don't want to be seen either. Anybody normal, well, I figured I'd duck in the bushes. Or tell them I was a guide. Or..." She shrugs, hopelessly. "I don't know. I tried not to think about it."

I look deep in her eyes. One of them's swollen again. "The beatings aren't from your auntie, are they? They're from 'working.'"

Esther shudders. She nods.

"Esther," I say, "I'm going to ask a very private question. But I really want the truth." I take a deep breath. "Do you use condoms?"

An uncomfortable pause. "I always bring some."

"That's not my question."

"It's not that simple," she pleads. "The guys don't like them. If I try to make them use them, they'll go to somebody else."

"Let them. Better that than get AIDS."

"What do you mean, get AIDS?" She stands up, really upset. "You make it sound like I'm a whore. I'm not. This is only for now. Once I get my brothers and sister back, things'll be different."

"How?"

"I don't know. They'll be different, that's all."

I laugh bitterly. "Your brothers and sister saw their mama and papa die. Now they'll see you die, too. That's *very* different. I'm sure they'll appreciate it, knowing you did it all for them."

"Go to hell!"

A car pulls up. The driver leans over. He could be somebody's grandpa. He motions us over with his hand.

Esther fixes me with a stare. "Suppose I do get AIDS. Suppose I die. So what? It can't be worse than this. Now get out of my way. I have work to do."

21

ALL NIGHT I HAVE BAD DREAMS. Esther's under that bridge in hooker park. She's pawed by old men who turn into skeletons.

She's chased by the living dead. She's crawling up a sewer pipe. Sores erupt all over her body.

I wake up terrified. My friend's going to be infected. She's going to get AIDS. I know it. I can't stop it. Nobody can. For all I know, it's already happened.

I recite like crazy—ABCDEFG—ABCDEFG—ABCDEFG— It doesn't work. My mind won't quit. I need to talk to somebody. But who? Kids at school would spread it around. Mama would make me stop seeing Esther.

I pray for help, but the words stick in my throat. "God, where are You?" I cry. "I want to believe, but You make it so hard."

I must have fallen asleep again because next thing I know Iris is shaking my shoulder: "Mama says get up or you'll be late for school."

Mama's already awake? I jump out of bed. Not only is Mama awake, she's in the kitchen making porridge. Is this another dream?

She sees me staring bug-eyed. "You've been doing far too much lately," she says. "Today it's my turn."

"Mama?"

"Don't ask me why, but I slept like a baby. Those herbs. It's amazing."

I try not to show too much excitement. Before class I check the encyclopedias in the school library. Sure enough, all the herbs Mr. Chilume gave Mama are listed. The encyclopedias say they're used in traditional medicines for digestion, fatigue and sleep disorders. Maybe Mr. Chilume isn't a quack after all.

After class I hurry home. I've gotten used to finding Mama in bed. Instead, today I find her sitting outside with Mrs. Tafa. She's wearing a fresh dress and a bright kerchief.

"Have a good day?" she asks. Her voice sparkles like I haven't heard in weeks.

"Really good," I say.

"Me too," she smiles. "I was just telling Mrs. Tafa, one day of treatment and I feel like a whole new person."

Mama's still unsteady on her feet, but she's got a lot more energy. Before supper she's able to chop potatoes for the soup, and afterwards to tell Iris and Soly a story using rags for hand puppets.

I'm not the only one to notice the change. Next day, Mrs. Tafa waves me over on my way to the standpipe. "Your mama's doing so much better," she whispers. "Yesterday, outside, talking. And this afternoon, why, I had her for a walk to the store."

"It's almost too good to be true!" I say, walking on air.

"'Oh ye of little faith,'" Mrs. Tafa nods smugly. "Dr. Chilume's a genius."

I bite my tongue. Whether Mama's recovery is because of Mr. Chilume's herbs—or Mama's belief in his herbs—it doesn't matter. She's starting to be Mama again. It's a miracle.

All week she makes progress. She spends more and more time outside, manages some errands, and best of all never stops smiling. I'm so happy I find myself singing for no reason.

The miracle comes to an end on Friday evening.

Mama's clearing plates after dinner. Out of the blue, she stiffens. The dishes crash to the floor. Mama sucks in her breath and grabs for a chair, her face frozen in pain. For a second she stands suspended. Then, she drops like a stone.

"Bed. Get me to bed." She clutches her head in agony.

Iris and Soly hide under the table as I drag Mama to her room. She's ripping the kerchief from her forehead. Now I see why she hasn't been rubbing her temples. It isn't because of the herbs. It's because of a tensor bandage. She's hidden it under her kerchief. Tied it so tight I'm surprised it hasn't taken her head off.

I watch in horror as her magical recovery vanishes before my eyes. Her energy's shriveled back up. She's small again. Frail.

"It's no use," she moans. "Nothing works. Not the herbs. Not anything."

"That's a lie," I cry. "You've had a spasm. That's all. You're getting better. You have to. For Iris. And Soly. And me. Please, Mama. Please. You've got to try."

"I *am* trying," she weeps. "I've been trying as hard as I can."

22

NEXT MORNING MAMA RESTS IN BED. When I go out to feed the chickens, I see Mrs. Tafa sipping lemonade. We nod, but we don't say anything. She knows.

Soly and Iris stay by Mama. Me, I keep outside, working hard so I won't have to think—about Mama, Esther, or anything. Late afternoon, I'm chopping firewood when Jonah's sister, Auntie Ruth, drives up with her boyfriend. Their rusty Corvette drags a two-wheeled wooden wagon. It stinks.

Auntie Ruth's boyfriend honks the horn and hollers: "End of the line!"

Auntie Ruth taps his arm. "Let me handle this." She gets out of the car. "Chanda, is your mama home?"

"She's sleeping."

"It's about Jonah."

"What about Jonah?"

Auntie Ruth bites her lip. "He came by our place near a month ago. Said he'd left your mama, needed a place to stay. We thought a day or two, he'd head back home. Instead he took to raving."

"He was probably drunk."

"It wasn't the drink."

Auntie Ruth's boyfriend gets out of the car. "We haven't got all day," he says. He grabs a pitchfork from the back seat and kicks the wagon so fierce the side boards shake. "You in there. Out, now—or I'll pitch you out like a bale of durra."

Iris and Soly stick their heads out the front door.

"Go back inside," I say.

"Yes, and get your mama!" Auntie Ruth shouts.

Mrs. Tafa gets up from her lawn chair. She peers over the hedge and calls Mr. Tafa to join her. Down the road, the Lesoles turn off their boom box and wander up for a look. Other neighbors collect, too. The Sibandas. Mr. Nylo the ragpicker. In fact, everyone we know.

Auntie Ruth's boyfriend waves the pitchfork over the end of the wagon. "Are you deaf?" he shouts. "I said, out!"

An unearthly wail from the wagon's floor. I look over the side boards.

"I'm sorry," Auntie Ruth says. "We can't keep him. He has to go."

I can't move. I can't speak. I can't take my eyes off the creature huddled in the corner. It's Jonah. No. It's what's left of Jonah. He's a skeleton. The flesh has been sucked out from under his skin. The skin's dried so tight to his skull that the bridge of his nose has ripped through. His striped bandanna has slipped from his forehead. It hangs around his neck like a noose. His old navy suit flows over his bones like rivers of cloth. Flies are eating him alive.

Auntie Ruth's boyfriend pokes him with the pitchfork. "I said out!"

"No!" Jonah shrieks. "Kill me!" He clutches the shaft of the pitchfork and tries to drive the spikes into his chest. "Don't leave me here! Kill me!"

Mama comes out of the house. She makes her way to the wagon, supported by her walking stick. At the sight of her, Jonah's so frightened he lets go of the pitchfork. He rises on stick legs and reels his head to our neighbors. "Two of my babies died in her belly. My baby Sara died from her milk." Sweat pours down his face. "I have good blood. Good seed. She laid a curse on me."

Auntie Ruth's boyfriend unhitches the wagon. It upends. Jonah topples back to the floor.

"Jonah, forgive me," Auntie Ruth weeps as she scrambles back into the car. Her eyes plead with Mama. "We have children of our own. It isn't safe." Her boyfriend revs the engine and the Corvette tears off, leaving the wagon with Jonah sprawled inside.

"Listen to me, Jonah," Mama says from the end of the wagon. "We'll get you to a doctor."

"I don't need no doctor." He claws his way over the side wall. "It's you that did this to me." He falls headfirst to the ground, wobbles back to his feet and squints into the crowd. He sees Mary hiding behind a cluster of neighbors, cap pulled low. "Mary? Is that you?" He totters toward her.

The crowd gasps. It pulls back. Mary tries to keep behind the Sibandas, but they grab her by the elbows and push her to the front.

"Mary, help me," Jonah begs.

"I don't know you!"

"Yes, you do. It's me. Jonah."

"No! You're a dead man! A scarecrow!"

"Please, Mary! You and me—"

"Keep away!" Mary cries in terror.

Jonah reaches out his arms to her.

"I'm warning you!" Mary grabs a fistful of stones. "Keep away!"

But Jonah doesn't listen. He staggers forward.

Mary whips the stones at his head. "Keep away! Keep away!"

The stones spray over Jonah's face. A cut opens over his left eye. He stops. Rocks back and forth in shock. His arms fall to his sides. He sinks to the ground, blinking back tears of blood. Then he covers his head with his hands and sobs.

The neighbors look away. There's an awful silence except for the sobbing. And then the voice of Mrs. Tafa: "Get yourself home, Leo," she yells to her husband. She's already indoors with her shutters closed.

Mr. Tafa lowers his head and shuffles off slowly. After a moment, so does everyone else. One by one they drift away, vanishing back inside their homes, until the entire road, and even the yards along the road, are empty.

Mary's the last to leave. "Sorry, old friend," she whispers to Jonah. "I didn't mean nothin'." Jonah howls, and suddenly Mary's running down the road as if her life depended on it.

Mama kneels beside him. Jonah won't look at her or speak. "You can stay out here or come inside," Mama says. "Either way, we'll bring you a blanket and a bowl of water."

She squeezes my arm and I help her to the house. Inside, she makes her way back to bed. "Can I leave you to take care of things?"

I'm not sure, but I nod. I try and remember what the doctor said at Esther's. When I bring the water and blanket to Jonah, I have my hands in plastic bags. Jonah has crawled under the wagon. He's curled in a ball, facing away from me. I put the water near his head. He shivers as I tuck the blanket around him.

"Rest easy," I say. He doesn't answer. His eyes are glassy. I'm not sure he even knows I'm there.

I hurry over to the Tafas and knock on the door.

"Stay still. She'll think we're out," I hear Mrs. Tafa whisper.

"I'm not deaf," I shout. "I know you're in there. Jonah's in a bad way. Can I use your phone to call a doctor?"

"Leave us out of this," Mrs. Tafa calls out. "It's none of our business."

"That's never mattered to you before!"

Never mind, I think. The hospital's not far. I let Mama know where I'm going, then hop on my bike and start to pedal. The air against my face feels good. My mind clears. But the second it does, the world floods in. My body trembles. I fall off my bike. I vomit at the side of the road.

Jonah has AIDS. And Jonah's slept with Mama.

I think about their dead babies.

And Mama's headaches. Her weariness. Her joints. The way she's gotten so thin. No wonder the herbs didn't work. Mama's problem isn't sleep or arthritis or fatigue. It's bigger. It's—

Mama! Please, God, no!

23

I BIKE THE REST OF THE WAY TO THE HOSPITAL, telling myself not to panic. Maybe Jonah got infected since Mama's last miscarriage. Maybe they'd stopped having sex. Maybe Mama's headaches are from grief, after all. Maybe she's all right.

Maybe.

I chain my bike to a link fence next to the hospital's emergency wing and run inside, almost knocking over a man on crutches. The lobby is packed. Even the window ledges are full. Women rock howling babies, men hold rags to open wounds, old folks squat on the floor, and screaming children run wild. Beyond, the corridors burst with stretchers: some surrounded by relatives, some covered in death sheets waiting to be taken to the morgue.

"Number 148?" The voice is coming from behind a counter. I see a sign that says Reception. A few dozen people bunch in front of it. I push my way through.

"I need an ambulance, right away," I say to the receptionist.

"Are you 148?"

"No. But this is an emergency!"

"So is this," she says, with a glance at the ward.

"I'm 148," says the woman behind me. Her face is covered in blisters.

I retreat and take a number from the peg on the nearby wall. Number 172. I'll be waiting forever.

Forever passes in a whir of orderlies, patients, nurses, cries, wails, buzzers, bells, and worries. When it's my turn, the receptionist buzzes me through the door beside her counter and into a room full of privacy screens and filing cabinets. Between the partitions, nurses are taking notes from patients and relatives. Some are hysterical.

I'm greeted by an older woman with wire-rim glasses. The

name tag on her uniform says "Nurse B. Viser." She leads me to her desk. It's covered in file folders, stacks of multi-colored forms, and a box of tissues. There's only one chair, a card table chair. She offers it to me and props herself against the end of the desk.

"If I could get a little personal information," she says, picking up a pen and clipboard.

I give her my name, age, street, and section number.

"Good," she smiles, and taps the end of her pen against her chin. "Now then, what can I do for you?"

I fill with fear. I can't say the problem out loud. I don't want it written down or connected to my family.

"A man's been beaten," I say. "He's bleeding under a wagon in front of my house."

"Have you called the police?"

"No. He doesn't need the police. He needs a doctor."

"I'm sorry," says Nurse Viser, "we don't have enough doctors for house calls. Call the police. If his injuries are serious, they'll bring him over."

"No, they won't," I say. "They won't touch him. They won't even go near him. Nobody will." I hold my breath and pray no one's listening. "He's very thin," I whisper.

Nurse Viser understands. She puts down her clipboard and takes my hand. "I'll put him on the list for a caseworker," she says. "But the earliest she can come is a week Monday. Your patient will still need a place to stay. There's no room for him here. Who are his family?"

"He doesn't have one anymore." My eyes begin to well. "And he won't come inside."

Nurse Viser hands me a tissue. "No, thank you," I say. "I'm

fine." I give directions to get to our house, and describe what it looks like so the caseworker can find it.

She writes it all down. "Until we can see him, make sure he's covered and given plenty of water."

"I've already done that."

"Good. The caseworker can give him an AIDS test to confirm your suspicions. In the meantime, be safe: use these whenever he needs changing." She reaches into a cupboard and hands me a box of rubber gloves.

I lower my eyes.

"It's hard, isn't it?" Nurse Viser says gently. She hugs me.

It's past sundown by the time I leave the hospital. The main strip is bright with neon lights, but the side streets are dark, except for the headlights of slow-moving cars trolling for hookers. The strip ends at the edge of downtown. I keep to the main roads, streaking through the patches of night that fall between the street lamps.

All the while, I think: should I have told Nurse Viser about Mama? About her problems? About my fears? I don't know. It's too confusing. Let sleeping dogs lie.

I reach my section. Something isn't right. It's too quiet for a Saturday. Where's the singing? The yard parties? Nowhere, that's where. Even the Lesoles' boom box is still. Two blocks from home, I spot a funeral tent. At last, I think, people. I ride up expecting to see some life. But the mourners sit around the firepit, frozen as corpses.

A cold knot grows in my stomach. It gets bigger the closer I get to home. A lamp glows in the main room. Soly and Iris are at the window, peeking out from between the slats of the shutters. Everything is as it should be. And yet...

Before heading in, I go to the wagon. Jonah's bowl is overturned by the yard-side wheel. I kneel and peer into the darkness underneath. "Jonah?"

I listen hard for a chatter of teeth, a whisper of breath, a rustle of blanket. Nothing.

"Jonah?" I say again.

A voice comes out of the night behind me. "Jonah's gone."

I whirl around. It's Mama.

"What are you doing out here?" I gasp.

"Waiting for you."

"Where's Jonah?"

"I don't know." Mama's voice is far away. "They say he wandered off at sundown."

"Who's 'they'?"

"Mrs. Tafa."

My mind races. "Oh my god, Mama, he's dead, isn't he? Somebody came back and did something."

"Why would anybody do anything? He left on his own. He wanted to go. To be alone. Mrs. Tafa said so." Mama leans heavily on her walking stick. "Now come inside," she says. "We've got a visitor."

24

OUR VISITOR IS MRS. GULUBANE. The local spirit doctor. She lives in the mopane hut across from the dump with her aging mama and a grown daughter, born without eyes.

Normally Mrs. Gulubane wears a cotton print dress, a kerchief, an old cardigan, and a pair of rubber sandals. But tonight is a business call. She has on her otterskin cap, her white robe with the crescent moons and stars, her red sash, and her necklace of animal teeth.

Our kitchen table and chairs have been pushed against the side walls. Mrs. Gulubane's reed mat has been unrolled in the center of the room. When I come in, she's sitting on it cross-legged. To her right is a whisk broom of yerbabuena stalks and a pot of water; to her left, a wicker basket and a handful of dried bones. This is how she presents herself on weekends at the bazaar, where she tells tourists their fortunes while her daughter hunches next to her weaving grass hats.

It's fun watching Mrs. Gulubane play with the tourists. Most traditional doctors try to keep their customers happy. Not Mrs. Gulubane. When she's in a bad mood, she'll tell them that their wives are cheating with the neighbors, and their children will be ripped apart by wild dogs. If they want their money back, her daughter rips the bandages off her eye sockets and threatens to attack them with her cane. It's amazing how fast tourists can run— even when they're loaded down with souvenirs and videocams.

Tonight, though, I'm not expecting fun. Here in the neighborhood, Mrs. Gulubane takes her rituals seriously. So do a lot of people—even people who know better. No matter what sounds come out of her hut, nobody ever says a word. I don't know how many people believe in her powers, but nobody wants to be at the end of her curse.

Mrs. Gulubane stays seated. "Good evening, Chanda." The lamplight shines off her two gold teeth.

I bow my head in respect, but what I'm thinking is: Why is she here?

She reads my mind. "There is bewitchment in this place. I have come to see what I can see."

I look uncertainly at Mama. Why did she ask her here? She doesn't believe in spirit doctors.

"It wasn't your mama called me," Mrs. Gulubane smiles. "I was sent for by a friend."

"Good evening, Chanda," comes a voice from the corner behind me. I turn. It's Mrs. Tafa. She closes the shutters.

Mrs. Gulubane indicates the floor in front of her mat. "Now that the family is together, shall we begin?"

Mama nods. She hands me her walking stick and takes my arm. I help her down and sit beside her. Soly and Iris squeeze between us. Mrs. Tafa sits in a chair; I suppose she's afraid if she sat on the floor she wouldn't be able to get up again.

Mrs. Gulubane lowers the lamp flame. Shadows dart up and down the walls. She takes an old shoe polish tin from her basket. Inside is a small quantity of greenish brown powder. She chants a prayer and rubs the powder between her fingers, sprinkling it into the pot of water. Then, stirring the water with the whisk brush, she dances about the room flicking a light spray into the corners, and over and under the windows and doorways.

I'm not sure what Mama is thinking, but Soly and Iris are frightened. "It's all right," I whisper. "It's just a show." Mrs. Gulubane stops in her tracks, tilts her ear toward us, and growls at the air. Soly buries his head in my waist.

Mrs. Gulubane returns to the mat. She pulls a length of red skipping rope from her basket, folds it in two, and begins to whip herself. Strange noises rattle up her throat. Spittle flies from her lips. Her eyes roll into her head. "HI-E-YA!" She throws back her arms, stiffens, and slumps forward in a heap.

A moment of silence. Then she sits up slowly and reaches for the bones. They're flat and worn, sliced from the ribs of a large animal. Mrs. Gulubane takes three in each hand. Chanting, she claps them together three times and lets them fall. She peers at the pattern they make. Something upsets her. She puts two of the bones aside. More chanting as she claps the remaining four and lets them fall. Her forehead knots tighter. She sets a second pair of bones aside and picks up the remaining two. A final chant. She claps them together. One breaks into three pieces in her hand. The fragments fall on the mat. She studies them closely, muttering heavily and shaking her head.

She looks up. Under the lamplight, Mrs. Gulubane's face contorts into the face of an old man. Her voice changes, too. It's low and guttural. She swallows air and belches words. "An evil wind is blowing from the north. There is a village. I see the letter 'T.'"

A pause. "Tiro," Mama says. Her voice is tired, resigned.

"Yes, Tiro. It is Tiro. Someone in Tiro wishes you harm."

"Only one?" asks Mama. I look over. Is there mockery in her voice?

Mrs. Gulubane glares. "No. More than one," she says. "But one above all others." She moves the bones around, cocks her head, and makes a deep whupping sound. "I see a crow. It hops on one claw."

Mrs. Tafa's breath seizes. "Lilian's sister has a clubfoot," she whispers from the corner.

Mrs. Gulubane claps her hands in triumph. "The bones are never wrong. This sister of yours," she says to Mama, "she has visited your home?"

"She came for the burial of my child," Mama replies. "And when I buried my late husband."

"Death. She has come for death," Mrs. Gulubane growls. "And to steal for her spells."

"Lizbet?" Mrs. Tafa gasps.

Mrs. Gulubane nods darkly. "When she has left, what things have been missing?"

"Nothing," Mama says.

"Nothing you remember. But maybe an old kerchief? An old hankie?"

"I don't know."

"The evil one is clever!" Mrs. Gulubane exclaims. "Each time she has come, she has taken a hankie, a kerchief, something so old it hasn't been missed. And she has snipped a braid of your hair—oh yes, each time a single braid—while you lay sleeping. With these she has bewitched you. She has put a spell on your womb. Even as we speak, the demon is coiled in your belly."

Without warning, Mrs. Gulubane lunges across the mat and punches her fist into Mama's guts. Mama howls in pain. The spirit doctor twists her fist back. Wriggling from her grip is a snake. She throws it against the wall and attacks it with Mama's walking stick.

The air is alive with magic. From every corner, animal noises blare, trumpet, and squawk. Mrs. Gulubane spins about, striking the reptile. Finally she leaps upon it, grabs it by head and tail and ties it in a knot. She lifts the lifeless body above her head. Its shadow fills the wall.

"I have killed this demon," she says. "But there will be others. The evil one has your hankies, your kerchiefs, your braids of hair, to make more spells. She has sewn the hankies into dollies, stitched on eyes and mouths, and filled them with cayenne. Therein the pain to your body. At night, she has singed your braids of hair. Therein the pain to your mind. Beware. You must retrieve what she has stolen or you and your children will surely die."

We stare in dumb silence as Mrs. Gulubane drops the snake into her pot, returns the pot, whisk brush, and tin to her basket, and rolls up her mat. She tucks the mat under her arm, takes the basket, and makes her way out the door.

Mrs. Tafa rushes after her. "For your troubles." She presses a few coins in Mrs. Gulubane's free hand. "Tomorrow, I'll have the family bring you two chickens for a sacrifice."

Mrs. Gulubane nods and vanishes into the night.

25

"WITCHCRAFT!" MRS. TAFA TURNS TO MAMA. "What did I tell you? We have to talk."

Mama gets up slowly and follows Mrs. Tafa outside. They huddle together on a pair of upturned pails. Mrs. Tafa waves her arms and babbles incoherently. Mama stares into the night.

Soly and Iris watch her from the front door. "Is it true?" they whisper. "Are we going to die?"

"No." I pull them back inside. "None of us is going to die."

"But Mrs. Gulubane said—"

"Mrs. Gulubane likes to hear herself talk."

"No," Iris gasps. "She talks to spirits!"

"She's a fake. Sorcery is just in books. At school, Mr. Selalame tells us all about how traditional doctors do their so-called magic."

"But the animal sounds—"

"Mrs. Gulubane makes them herself. It's a cheap ventriloquist's trick."

"But the snake—"

"Hidden in a pocket up her sleeve."

"Then why didn't her sleeve wriggle?"

"The snake was dead the whole time. She made it look alive the way she flicked it with Mama's stick."

"But—"

"But But But But But!" I explode. "You're not going to die, and that's all there is to it. Now brush your teeth and go to bed!"

As I tuck them in, I curse Mrs. Gulubane. And I curse Mrs. Tafa for bringing her. Thanks to those old crows, Soly will be peeing his diaper forever. I give them a big hug and a kiss. "I'm sorry I yelled at you."

"That's okay," Iris says. For a change, her arms stay tight around my neck. "Chanda, please don't get mad again—but if Mrs. Gulubane is a fake, why does Mama believe in her?"

"Mama doesn't believe in her," I say. "Mama just pretended to believe in her so she'd go away."

Iris considers this. "If Mama was just pretending," she whispers, "why is she still outside with Mrs. Tafa?"

"She's being polite."

Iris frowns. So does Soly.

"Would you like a lamp?" I ask.

They nod.

By the time I have them settled, Mama's come in and gone to her room. The curtain is drawn across her doorway.

"Mama?"

When she doesn't say anything, I peek inside. She's crumpled on her mattress. A pillowcase stuffed with clothes is sitting next to her.

"I'm going to Tiro tomorrow," she says.

I clutch the door frame. "What?"

"I have to. Mrs. Gulubane read the bones."

"No, she didn't. She repeated gossip. Things she could have heard from Mrs. Tafa or anybody."

Mama rubs her temples. "This house is bewitched."

"You don't believe that."

"Don't I?" Mama dares me. "Then look me in the eye and tell me why my Sara died. Tell me why my Jonah is dying. Tell me why my joints ache and my head splits apart."

My mind burns with the truth. I long to take the dare—but saying it will make it real. Here. Now.

"Mrs. Tafa's offered to keep an eye out," Mama says. "She'll help you with Iris and Soly."

"No, Mama. You're not going anywhere. You're not well enough."

"Nonsense. The fresh air will do me good."

I'm about to beg when I smell smoke. Hear a crackling of burning wood. It's coming from the front of the house. I race to the window of the main room. The wagon by the road is ablaze.

I run into the yard, Mama beside me, Soly and Iris too. The street is empty. Whoever did this has fled into the night. I look to Mrs. Tafa's house. Her shutters are closed. So are the shutters of all the neighbors up and down the street. They're watching from the darkness—I can feel it—but none of them come out.

Mama throws back her shoulders like she did the day we left Isaac Pheto's. She tosses away her cane. "Let the wagon burn," she says. She turns as powerful as a queen in the firelight and leads us back into the house.

Once Soly and Iris have been comforted back to bed, she collapses. I sit at the side of her bed and hold her hand.

"You see, Chanda?" she says. "It doesn't matter what I believe. Mrs. Gulubane has paid us a visit. If I don't go to Tiro like she says, who knows what some lunatic may do next?"

26

Saturday night turns to Sunday morning.

We sit at the kitchen table eating our porridge in silence. I clear the dishes and Mama tells Soly and Iris she has an important announcement. Before she can say another word, Iris says: "You're going away, aren't you?"

"Just for a little," she nods.

Iris turns to Soly. "I told you." She shoves her chair away from the table and heads to the front door.

"Iris, come back, I haven't finished," Mama says.

Iris ignores her. She flounces outside and flops cross-legged on the ground.

I get up. "Mama's talking to you, Iris."

Iris pays no attention. She talks to the chickens who strut around looking for feed. I'm about to drag her back in, but Mama stops me.

Meanwhile, tears roll down Soly's cheeks. They drip off his chin. He doesn't bother to wipe them.

Mama wraps her arms around him. "It's only a trip," she comforts.

His little shoulders heave. "When people go on trips, they don't come back."

"Well, *I'm* coming back. I just have to see some relatives in Tiro. Isn't that right, Chanda?"

"Absolutely."

Soly's eyes are so big I think they'll fall out of his head. "Promise?"

"Promise." Mama kisses his forehead. "While I'm gone, Chanda will be in charge. She'll need your help. Can you help her for me?"

He nods, his breath catching as if it's all too much to bear.

"There's nothing to worry about," Mama continues. "If worst comes to worst, Mrs. Tafa's next door with her phone."

"When will you be back?" he asks.

"A few days. Maybe a week."

A pause. "How long before you go?"

"This afternoon sometime. After the cemetery tour."

"Can I go with you?"

"Tiro's pretty far for a little man."

"No, but to the cemeteries. I want to be with you as long as I can. Please? Chanda gets to go. Why not Iris and me?"

Mama looks to me.

"They're old enough." I shrug. "Besides, it might help somebody deal with S–a–r–a."

Mama fetches Mrs. Tafa for the cemetery tour, while I get Soly and Iris ready. I thought this would be an adventure for them— a sign they were all grown-up—but Iris stays bratty: "I don't want to go to any cemeteries."

"If you come, you can wear your Sunday School dress."

"I hate my Sunday School dress."

"No, you don't."

"Yes, I do. It's not really mine, anyway. It's from the church bin. It's somebody else's who didn't want it. I don't want it either."

I cross my arms. "Iris, you're coming and that's that. Now get up and get moving."

Iris stops arguing. In fact, she stops doing everything. She stands in her room like a rag doll and makes me dress her, one arm and leg at a time. I even have to bend her knees and elbows.

She's no easier on the drive. Mama talks privately with Mrs. Tafa in the cab, while Iris, Soly, and I squat on the flatbed. For once, Mrs. Tafa drives like a human being. Maybe she's quiet on account of Mama's conversation, or what happened last night, or not wanting to send us kids flying. Whatever the reason, I only have to knock twice on the rear window to get her to slow down.

The ride distracts Soly. He points at birds and waves when we pass children traveling by foot, bike, and buggy. Head over the side of the flatbed, the wind in his face, he's king of the county. Iris, on the other hand, is queen of the grumps. She doesn't even get excited when we pass a three-legged dog running around a warthog.

At Papa's cemetery, I lift Soly off the flatbed. I go to help Iris down, but she refuses to budge. "Why can't I stay in the truck? He's not *my* papa."

"Do it for Mama and me."

She wrinkles her face. "My stomach hurts."

She's the same at Mr. Dube's. Even at Sara's.

Mama gathers us around Sara's marker. "This is where your sister lives," Mama says. "This is where we come to be with her and to remember happy times."

While Soly copies everything Mama does, Iris acts like she couldn't care less. She rocks on her heels. I yank her out of earshot.

"Show some respect," I say. "Sara's resting there."

"No, she isn't," Iris says. "Sara's someplace else." In a quiet singsong voice, she chants: "*I know something you don't know. I know something you don't know.*"

"If Sara isn't there," I say, "where do you think she is?"

She puts a finger to her lips. "It's a secret. I promised her I wouldn't tell."

I thought Iris's imaginary friend had disappeared, but she's back with a vengeance. I want to tell Mama. I should. But I can't. The worry would drive her crazy. A hole opens in the pit of my stomach. I bottle up the terror.

Back home, Iris, Soly, and I wait with Mama for the bus. The wagon's stopped smoking, but there's a smell of charred wood in the air.

Mama pretends not to notice. She tells stories to make us laugh. We try, to make her happy, but laughing's too hard. Even breathing is hard. Soly looks like he's going to cry. Mama catches him. "Soly, what did I tell you?"

"'Never let them see you cry,'" he whispers.

"That's right," she says gently, wiping a tear from his eye. "You can cry in the house. But not outside. People will think something's wrong. We don't want that, do we?"

He shakes his head.

"Good." Mama adjusts his jacket. "If you feel the tears coming, just close your eyes and tell yourself a story. A little dream can make the world a happier place." She looks at us solemnly. "Now, one last time before I go: People may tease you about why I'm away. If neighbors ask questions, what do you say?"

"Everything's fine," we repeat dully. "Mrs. Gulubane's solved everything. She's sent you to Tiro to break a spell."

"And what do you say to people who don't believe in traditional doctors?"

"You're staying with our sister Lily. She's had a new baby. You're helping her out."

"Good."

The Tafas' screen door bangs shut. We look over to see Mrs. Tafa coming our way. She's hauling a picnic basket in one hand and a shopping bag in the other. "Lilian, I must be losing my mind," she pants. "You're almost away and I forgot to give you these."

She plants the bag and basket at our feet. First she raises the checked cotton cloth covering the picnic basket. Inside are things from the tourist shops—things we'd never be able to afford. Jams, jellies, chocolate bars, tinned meats, canned apples, fancy skin lotions and perfumes, and a bottle of aspirin.

"You don't want to show up at your relatives empty-handed," Mrs. Tafa says. She reaches into the shopping bag and pulls out a brand-new dress. It's a bright yellow covered in blue parakeets. "I want you to change into this at the last rest stop. If you don't mind my saying so, the dress you're wearing has seen its days."

"Oh, Rose," Mama says, "this is too generous."

"Nonsense. Your Joshua always wanted you in new clothes, remember?"

I want to give Mrs. Tafa a hug. I want to kiss her for being so good to Mama. But after Mama's thank-yous and five minutes of chitchat, I start wanting her to disappear. She's taking over our final good-byes with Mama—time worth more than all the jams and jellies in the world. I stare at her hard, to drill thoughts into her head. Thoughts like: "Go away, you stupid cow. We need Mama for us. Just for us."

Mrs. Tafa doesn't get the message. Instead, she settles in. My stomach heaves, knowing she'll be here till Mama's gone.

"I've put Chanda in charge," I hear Mama say. "But I've said that if there's a problem you're right next door."

"That's right," Mrs. Tafa beams at Iris and Soly. "Your Auntie Rose will take care of you."

"Thank you, Mrs. Tafa," I say. "But I'm sure I can manage." I'm not sure at all. In fact, I'm scared sick. But I don't want Mrs. Tafa barging around with her nose in our business.

Mama's bus arrives.

We all get up except Iris. Mama kneels down and gives her a hug. Iris hangs limp. Not Soly. He gives her a world of hugs. "I miss you already." He closes his eyes tight.

I help Mama to her feet. She grips my arms. "I'm counting on you," she says, searching my eyes. "Keep them safe. Make me proud."

"I promise."

She gives me a squeeze. The driver and I help her onto the back of the truck. Mrs. Tafa passes up her bundle and the basket and shopping bag.

"Don't you worry, Lilian," Mrs. Tafa says. "I'll keep an eye on everything."

Mama smiles and ignores her. "I'll be back soon," she waves to us. "I love you."

And she's gone.

PART THREE

27

THE REST OF THE DAY IS STRANGE. When I pretend Mama's inside resting, everything seems normal. But when I think of her on a bus hundreds of miles away, my insides ache to bursting.

I have to talk to Iris. About her behavior. About her wild talk at the cemetery. But what do I say? What would Mama say? I don't know. I can't think. This is crazy. Lately I've done all the work around the house. But Mama was here in case I made a mistake. Without her, even the simplest chores seem enormous. I'm almost afraid I can't boil water. What'll I do if something important goes wrong?

Before supper, Mrs. Tafa drops over with a chicken pie. She tries to act light-hearted, but it's like she's bringing food to a burial feast.

"What did Mama tell you in the truck?" I ask.

"Nothing for you to worry about," she says and hurries off.

The pie is good, but none of us eats much. After sundown, I put Iris and Soly to bed and tell them the story about the impala and the baboon. Then I go outside and sit on the ground, propping my back against the side of the house. The stars are clear. Most nights I think how beautiful they are. Tonight they just look cold and far away.

The loneliness makes it hard to breathe. I try to get up, but my knees won't let me. I wish the earth would swallow me up. It's now, when everything feels so completely hopeless, that I realize I'm not alone. A stork is peering at me from beside the wheelbarrow. Its white feathers glow in the moonlight.

I can't believe my eyes. Storks sleep at night. And they don't come into town. They stay near water where they can feed on fish. How far has this one traveled? At this time of year, the likeliest spots are the marshes around the Kawkee dam. But they're miles away!

I whisper greetings. "Dumêla, mma moleane."

The stork tilts its neck. If I didn't know better, I'd say it was smiling.

"What brings you here?"

The stork cocks its head to one side.

"Are you a good-luck angel?" As I hear the words come out of my mouth, I feel foolish. I'm too old for make-believe. But the stork doesn't care. It takes two steps toward me and pauses, its leg in the air, while it considers a third.

We stare at each other. Time disappears. I feel the world turn calm. My shoulders melt. I close my eyes. I see Mama, big the way she used to be. Her arms cradle me. I hear the sound of her laughter, rich and round. My heart glows with her warmth.

When I wake, the stork is gone. It doesn't matter. The joy of my dream flickers inside me like fireflies. I smile, rub my eyes, and stretch. Then I go inside, taking care to tiptoe so I won't wake my babies. My babies—that's what they've become, my brother and sister. At the door to the bedroom I hear them whispering to each other under their sheet. I stay very still and listen.

"Chanda's papa's dead," Iris is saying. "Your papa, too. But my papa's alive."

My heart stops. Iris knows about Isaac Pheto, but she's never talked about him. Tonight's different. "*My* papa's alive," she whispers again to Soly. "If everybody dies, I'm going to live with him."

"How do you know he'd want you?" Soly whispers back.

"He tells me. He has a great big house and he says I can have any room I want. Just for me."

"Liar. You never even see him."

"I do too."

"Where?"

"At kindergarten. He visits all the time and takes me for rides in his big yellow car. He buys me ice cream. He flies an airplane. He's very rich. He's the biggest boss at the mine."

"So why doesn't he ever come here?" Soly challenges.

"Because of Mama. She ran away with your papa. But your papa died, so 'ha ha' on her."

"That's mean."

"So what?"

Soly gets very quiet. "Iris... if everybody dies and you leave with your papa... what'll happen to me?"

"How should I know?"

Soly begins to sniffle. "Take me with you?"

"We'll see. But only if you stop peeing the bed."

I stick my head in. "Is everything all right?"

Soly's about to say something, but Iris kicks him under the sheet. "We're fine. Soly's just lonesome."

"Me too," I say. I wait, hoping they'll say more, but they don't. "'Night then. I'll be coming in to bed soon."

"Night."

The minute I'm gone, Iris whispers to Soly: "Keep your mouth shut about what I said, or I'll tell my papa and you'll be all alone forever."

28

NEXT DAY AFTER DOING THE BREAKFAST DISHES, I walk Soly over to Mrs. Tafa's hedge. She told Mama she'd look after him in the morning while Iris and I are in school. She offered to look after Iris in the afternoon too, but on account of Iris's imaginary friend, I've decided to stay home to watch her.

Soly's been very quiet this morning. I think about what Iris told him. On the way to the hedge I make him stop, and pretend to wipe some dirt from his nose. "In case anybody ever tells you different," I say, "you'll never be alone. Mama loves you and she'll be home soon. Mrs. Tafa loves you and she's right next door. I love you and I'm not going anywhere."

A pause. Soly looks up. He grins shyly: "Except to school."

"Except to school."

"And except to the standpipe."

"And except to the standpipe."

"And except to—"

I knuckle his head and pass him over the hedge to the waiting arms of Mrs. Tafa. Then I go back, pack my schoolbooks in my carrier, and adjust Iris's combs.

"My braids are too tight," she whines.

"Want me to make them tighter?" I give the combs a little twist and she shuts up.

I walk her to kindergarten, rolling my bike between us. Iris acts like I don't exist. When we near the playground, I say: "Soly was very upset last night. Were you making up stories?"

"None of your business."

"Everything's my business."

"You're not Mama!" she taunts.

"Yes, I am," I say. "While she's away, I make the rules. That's rule number one. Rule number two: Be nice to Soly. Rule number three: Be home right after school. No excuses."

"Make me." She tosses her head and runs over to a group of friends.

I want to yank her back by the hair. But then what? If she runs off laughing, I'll look like a fool. But if I do nothing I'll *be* a fool. I see her skipping. I do nothing. I'm a coward.

The early bell rings. I'm nearly late for my own school. I take a quick look for her teacher, Mrs. Ndori. Maybe I can ask her to keep a special eye out. I check at the office. She hasn't arrived yet. I can't wait. Maybe it wouldn't have done any good anyway. Mrs. Ndori went into teaching when her husband died. She has a heart of gold, that's about it. Her students run wild. There's a rumor she drinks.

I get to class just in time. My hardest subjects—math, physics, and chemistry—are in the morning. The ones I'm good at— English, history, and geography—are in the afternoon when I'll be home. Skipping shouldn't be a problem.

At lunch, I knock on the staff room door.

I'm not sure what my teachers have heard about the week-end commotion. If they gossip about students like we gossip about them, they've probably heard plenty. Thankfully, they don't let on.

I tell them I have to be away. They're sympathetic, but concerned. "So many students only plan to miss a week or two," Mr. Selalame says. "Then it turns into a month. Then they drop out. You're so close to graduating, Chanda. So close to a scholarship. Take care. I worry about you."

"Well, don't. I won't let you down. I have dreams, remember?"

There aren't enough textbooks for me to have my own, but there's a copy of each one in the library. I promise to come early and do the readings before morning class. Also to do all the assignments at home. If there are special tests and exams, well, hopefully Mama will be back by then.

Mr. Selalame gives me a bookmark with a picture of a ripe sun rising over the plains. "If you need any extensions, just ask."

The talk with my teachers takes longer than expected. As I bike past the elementary school, I see morning classes are already out. I pedal fast, expecting to catch up with Iris, but she's nowhere to be seen. I get a horrible feeling. The second I'm home, I drop my bike and race in the door.

"Iris?"

She's not inside.

"Iris??"

Did I push her too hard?

"Iris???"

Did she run away? Have I messed up? I barrel outside in a panic.

Mrs. Tafa waves at me from across the hedge. "Chanda, yoo hoo. Iris is over here. She and Soly are having a bowl of seswa."

I hop the hedge. Iris is sitting on the ground beside Mrs. Tafa's lawn chair, munching happily. "You're late," Iris says.

"I had to talk to my teachers."

"Oh," she replies smugly. "I didn't think excuses were allowed."

My insides boil. But what makes it worse—Mrs. Tafa laughs. "What a sharp one," she hoots. "Quick as a whip."

Iris bats her eyes and snuggles closer to Mrs. Tafa.

"By the way," Mrs. Tafa continues, "your mama called from the general dealer's to say she arrived in Tiro safe and sound."

"When'll she be calling next?"

"She didn't say. But don't you worry. I'll pass on any messages."

"Thanks, but I'd like to talk to her myself."

Mrs. Tafa considers my request. "Well, if you're home," she says.

I walk Iris to school for the rest of the week, but keep missing Mrs. Ndori. I finally bump into her on the playground Friday morning. "I've been away sick with a cold," she apologizes, blowing her nose. "The teacher in the next classroom has watched the children, though. I'm sure everything's been fine."

"I hope so," I say. "But I'm not here about that." I explain how Iris has been difficult lately and hand her a piece of paper with my name, and Mrs. Tafa's phone number. "Could you please call me if you notice anything unusual?"

Mrs. Ndori squints at the paper. She seems a bit confused. "Certainly," she says, and sneezes. She wipes her nose and crumples the paper into her jacket pocket along with a wad of tissues. A stray soccer ball bonks her on the back of the head. "Boys!" she hollers and storms off to scold a crowd of children pointing at her and laughing.

Sunday, Iris and Soly watch Mr. Tafa fix the thatching on his tenants' roofs, while Mrs. Tafa and I do the cemetery tour. She tells me funny stories from our days at the mine. Without Mama here to laugh it's not the same. I sit quietly while her stories turn to her son Emmanuel.

"Such a clever boy. When he was little, he tried to teach Meeshak and me how to read, so we could read him bedtime stories. We never got the knack of it. Not like your mama. Oh my, so gifted. All those brains. I don't know where he got them from." Mrs. Tafa wipes her eyes with her hankie. "There's so much dust around here."

She drives me to the Macholo gravesite. For the second week in a row, Esther's nowhere to be seen. I know Mrs. Tafa's dying to lecture me about Esther being a bad influence, but she doesn't. Why is she being so nice? It makes me nervous.

"It's been a week. Mama should be back by now," I say.

"Child, the more you want to hurry life up, the slower it gets." Mrs. Tafa braces herself and hits the accelerator.

After supper, I sit out front and listen to the music blasting from the Lesoles' boom box down the road. Mr. Lesole's on an extended leave from the safari camp and he's making the most of it. Mrs. Tafa comes over to the hedge.

I imagine she'll say what she always says: "Those Lesoles and their street parties. They should keep it down once in awhile, so folks can make music someplace else."

But tonight she surprises me.

"You should get yourself down there, girl. No sense you dragging about like a cart with no wheels." She sees me hesitate. "Go on now. I'll watch the children. You have yourself some fun. You don't want folks thinking there's a problem here, do you?"

She's right. When folks think there's a problem, they talk. I put on my cheeriest face, and head down the road. Before I know it, I'm at the Lesoles, surrounded by laughter and dance. "Dumêla!" Mrs. Lesole calls out, bouncing over to embrace me.

"Dumêla!" Mr. Lesole pipes as well. "We hear your mama's up north."

"Yes," I shout over the music. "She's gone to help my big sister with her new baby."

"Good for her," Mrs. Lesole shouts back. "New mamas need all the help they can get." She gives her husband an affectionate elbow.

"Your mama's so lucky! All that fresh country air!" Mr. Lesole adds heartily.

Their next-door neighbor comes up to show off his new kite. He's made a long, shiny tail out of pop-can tabs. We all admire it, and then I mingle through a crowd of friendly neighbors. It's like that day with Jonah never happened.

At last it's time to go. By the open gate I find Mr. Nylo sitting in a wheelbarrow with a bag of freshly collected rags. He gives me an excited wave. "I hear everything's fine with your mama," he says. "Mrs. Tafa's passed the word."

"Yes!" I exclaim. "Everything's fine!" As I head home, music ringing in my ears, dances tickling my toes, I almost believe it.

If only she'd call.

I'm not the only one waiting for Mama to call. Before supper on Monday, Soly's sitting at the side of the road. He's been going there to wait for Mama ever since she left.

I watch him from the window. He sits patiently. Then a butterfly will flutter by and he'll chase it. Or he'll squat down and stare at an anthill or do a somersault. Or make up a song.

That's what he's doing now as I sneak up behind him. It's a simple song: "Oh, I'm waiting, I'm waiting, I'm waiting, I'm waiting, I'm sitting here waiting for Mama, just sitting here waiting for Mama, just sitting here waiting, and waiting, and waiting..."

Hearing his thin, tiny voice waver in the breeze overwhelms me. Soly catches me listening. He stops singing, and stares at the ground as if he's been doing something bad.

"What's the matter?" I sit beside him.

A pause. Then he says in a quiet voice, "I was singing."

"I know. It was nice."

"It was?"

I nod.

His forehead wrinkles up with questions. "You mean it's all right to sing...to play...to have fun...with Mama gone?"

"Yes." I squeeze him. "Mama wants us to be happy."

Another pause. "Chanda...why hasn't she called again?"

"Maybe she doesn't have anything to say."

Soly stares at his toes. "Do you think she misses us?"

"Of course she misses us. Just like we miss her." I kiss his forehead. "Don't worry. No news is good news."

Soly tries to smile, but he can't. He doesn't believe me. Why should he? I don't believe me either.

29

WAITING FOR MAMA IS STRANGE. Sometimes I fill with hope. Other times, like tonight, I lie in bed sweating with terror.

Soly is right. Mama should have called again. What's wrong? Is her sickness worse?

Her AIDS, I mean. Why can't I say the truth even now? Who am I trying to fool? How long before she dies? How long before we're alone? What then?

I see Jonah's face. I flash with hate. He gave it to her. I know it. I hope he's dead in some ditch. Stinking. Rotting.

No. That's awful. Anyway, why think the worst? Mama hasn't been tested. I don't know anything for sure. *Maybe* she has AIDS. But maybe not.

"Mama doesn't have AIDS. Mama doesn't have AIDS." I say it over and over. But I don't believe it. Instead, I get a more terrible thought: What if Mama has AIDS, but not from Jonah? What if she gave it to him?

No! I hit myself. But the idea won't go away. It itches and itches.

I calm down. I tell myself not to be stupid. If Mama didn't get AIDS from Jonah, then from who? From nobody, that's who.

Then I think of Mr. Dube. He was a widower for a long time. Did he spend all those nights alone? Or was there a trip to a boxcar? A stroll to hooker park?

No. Mr. Dube was nice.

So what? Nobody's perfect. People make mistakes. They do things they shouldn't. That they normally wouldn't. That they wish they hadn't.

I start to sweat. If Mr. Dube gave Mama AIDS—then what about their baby? What about Soly?

No! If Soly had the virus, he would have died before Sara! Wouldn't he?

Maybe not. By the time Sara was born, Mama would've had it longer. Sara could've been born sicker.

Oh no, an even worse thought: What if Mama didn't get sick from Jonah or from Mr. Dube? What if she got sick from Isaac Pheto?

Then what about *their* baby? What about Iris?

My heart stops. What about me?

I think of what Isaac did to me. The times he did it. I thought that was my one big secret. But what if there's another secret? What if Isaac gave me AIDS?

ABCD-CD-CD-CDEG-GF-FG—I can't even remember the alphabet.

I get up, walk around, go back to bed. Get up, walk around, go back to bed. Get up, walk around, go back to bed. All the while, reciting, reciting, reciting—but instead of letters I'm reciting every cold I ever had. Every fever. Every headache. Every diarrhea. I think of all the times I couldn't sleep, the times I sweated in the middle of the night. Was it normal? Or symptoms?

Please God, help me. Tell me I'm all okay. Tell me. But He doesn't. I'm swallowed up by silence.

The torture goes on till I'm too tired to be frightened. My head hits the pillow, and I fall into a world of other nightmares.

I dream I'm at the junkyard. I'm not sure how I got here. All I know is I'm alone, it's night, and I'm lost in a maze of tires and broken pots piled to the sky.

"Chanda?" a voice calls. It's a ghost voice, light as air.

"Who are you?"

It doesn't say. It just keeps calling me. "Chanda? Chanda?"

It leads me through the maze to the abandoned well. "Help me, Chanda," the voice floats up from down below. "Please? Help me?"

I'm rolling over in bed, half awake now, the dream voice still in my ears. "Chanda?" A light tapping on the window shutters.

I sit up. Dreams can take us into the future. This one comes from right now. "Esther?" I whisper.

There's a whimpering. I run to the front door, undo the bolt, and open it. Esther comes around the corner of the house. She stays in the shadows, out of the light of the moon: "Stay back. Don't look at me."

"What's happened?"

A moan so horrible I think the earth will open up. I run to her, but she holds up her hand. "No. It isn't safe."

I catch a glimpse. I pull back. "Esther..." I say, as calmly as I can. "Esther, come inside."

"I can't. Your mama..."

"She's not here. You have to come inside."

She follows me in. Soly and Iris have woken up. I tell them to stay in their room. I draw the bedroom curtain and light the lamp. Esther collapses to the floor. She's battered, swollen, and half-naked. Her halter top and mini-skirt are ripped. Caked in dirt, dried blood, and pus. Her face is slashed. Stitches run from her forehead over her nose and down to her throat.

"We have to get you to a hospital."

"I've already been. The doctors were busy. A nurse sewed me up. She said I was lucky I didn't lose an eye. But there'll be scars." A terrible sob.

"They should have given you a bed."

"There weren't any. Besides, I'm just a whore."

"No, you're not. You're my friend. My best friend."

Esther buries her face in her hands and cries.

I put on a pair of the rubber gloves I got from Nurse Viser, and bring over the breakfast water. There's some antiseptic in a bottle under the sink. I bring that, too, as well as a few clean rags, my housecoat, and a blanket. I help Esther out of her torn clothes. There're bruises everywhere. Even behind her ears and on her back. I dab antiseptic on the nicks and cuts the nurse overlooked.

"Chanda... Chanda, I never thought this would happen. To other people maybe. Not to me. I'm such a fool." She starts to shiver. I get her into my housecoat.

"Shh, shh," I say. "You don't have to explain."

Esther wipes her eyes. "I do. I need to. You're the only one I can tell." She's shaking now. I bundle her in the blanket and rock her. Her words pour out in little gasps. "It was a slow night. A trick at the mall, one in the park, that's it. Then, ten o'clock, a limo pulls up, tinted windows and everything. The driver says, 'There's a party at the Safari Club. Twenty bucks plus tips, you interested?'

"I say, 'Sure.' I open the door to the back seat. Two men in masks are inside waiting for me. I try to run, but the driver's behind me. He grabs me, shoves me in. One of the men says, 'Scream and you die.' The other ties a pillowcase over my head.

"We drive and drive. We stop I don't know where, a garage maybe. I hear other men circle the car. The door opens. I'm dragged out. Held down. And then they all come at me. It goes on and on. They whistle and laugh. The last one says, 'I got AIDS from a whore. Now I'm giving it to you.' They toss me in the car trunk. I'm sure I'm going to die. Next thing I know, I'm in a ditch. A masked man rips the pillowcase off my head. 'Remember me when you look in the mirror,' he says. He slashes my face. They drive away."

Esther and I huddle together, very still, for a long time.

"The cops found me," she says at last. "All the way to the hospital, they asked questions. I didn't have any answers. I only saw the driver. It was night. He was in shadow. The limo was just a limo. I don't even know where they took me." She chokes. "The cops didn't care about that part anyway. They wanted to know why I was out so late: 'You a whore?' they asked. Like I deserved it."

"Nobody deserves this," I say. "Nobody."

"Tell that to my auntie. After the hospital, the cops took me to her place. She said it was my own fault, I was a slut and I'd burn in hell. Then she kicked me out. I went to the shed. Put my stuff in a bag. Biked here, I don't know how. My bag's at the side of the house."

Esther's overcome. She gulps breath after breath. "Chanda..." she says, "Chanda, I have nowhere to go."

"Yes, you do," I say, holding her tight. "You have here. You have right here."

30

I PUT ESTHER IN MAMA'S ROOM, exchanging Mama's mattress for my own. Soly's fallen back to sleep, but as I make the switch I catch Iris peeking at me from under the sheet. How much did she hear? How much did she understand?

"So she's staying," Iris whispers.

I nod. Iris groans and rolls over.

I go back to Mama's room and tuck Esther in.

"I'm never going to sleep again," she says. But she does. Her breathing's heavy. Her body twitches. I hope her dreams take her to a happier place.

Mine don't. When I finally get to bed, I dream I'm back at the junkyard. Voices call to me from the abandoned well. Mama. Sara. Iris. Soly. Esther. "Help us, Chanda, help us," they cry. I lean over the lip of the well. "I can't," I cry. "I don't know how." A wind blows me over the side. I'm falling. Falling and falling and—out of nowhere a giant white bird, my magic stork, swoops down and catches me in its bill. It holds me safe and flies me into the sky. I see storm clouds in the distance. "Where are we going?" I ask. "What lies ahead?" But before the stork can answer I find myself sitting up in bed, wide awake.

Esther's still asleep when Soly and Iris come to breakfast.

Soly pads to the table scratching his bum. "Is it true Esther's staying with us?"

"Yes." I glance at Iris. "News travels fast."

Iris stirs her porridge with a know-it-all smile. "Tell Soly why she's staying."

"Esther had an accident," I lie. "She fell off her bike onto some glass. She was stuck in a toolshed at her auntie's. This is a better place for her to heal."

"Tell Soly the real reason."

"That is the real reason," I say evenly. (At least it's *half-true*, I think. And half-true is more true than most things around this place.)

Soly rubs his eyes. "How long will she be here?"

"As long as she wants."

"Does Mama know?" Iris asks innocently.

"She will," I whisper. "She won't mind either. Even if she

did, she'd be polite. She likes guests to feel welcome. Unlike one little brat I could mention."

Iris ignores me. "Soly," she smiles sweetly, "would you like my porridge? It's got bugs."

"Don't listen to her. She's lying."

"I am not."

Soly puts down his spoon.

After we clear the dishes, I walk him to Mrs. Tafa's hedge. She's waiting with open arms. "Guess what?" Soly whoops as I pass him across. "Esther's living at our place!"

Mrs. Tafa nearly drops him on the cactus. (I wish she had.) "Esther Macholo?"

"Un-hunh," he nods happily. "She fell off her bike and now she's staying in Mama's bedroom."

Mrs. Tafa arches an eyebrow. "Is this some kind of joke?"

"No," I say. "Esther's having a rough time. If it's all right, when I get home, I'd like to use your phone to call the general dealer in Tiro. You know, to let Mama know."

"You don't want to be upsetting your mama."

"This won't upset her."

Mrs. Tafa cranes her neck as though I'm an idiot.

"Anyway," I say nervously, "I have to run. I promised my teachers I'd get to school early. I have to do a makeup test in physics, hand in an English essay, and, well, good-bye."

Mrs. Tafa's about to stop me, but Soly tugs at her dress. "Mrs. Tafa," he says, "can I get a glass of lemonade? My porridge had bugs."

I drop Iris off at kindergarten. This morning I didn't have time to think. Now that I'm alone, I'm drowning in nightmares. Real ones.

What'll I do if Esther gets sick? Or if Iris runs away? Or if Mama dies? Or if Auntie Lizbet swoops in? Or if I have AIDS? WHAT'LL I DO IF I HAVE AIDS???

I have to talk to someone. Who? Mr. Selalame! When I get to school I'll talk to Mr. Selalame—he'll know what to do.

Mr. Selalame! Yes! I pedal fast.

Mr. Selalame! No! He's a teacher. He'll have to write a report. What if it leaks out? I'll be the AIDS girl with the AIDS mama and the AIDS friend. What if the city finds out? What if they take Soly and Iris away? Would they? Could they? I don't know.

I forget about school. I head to the hospital. I give my name to reception and ask for Nurse Viser. Eventually she sticks her head out. She waves me in.

"We sent a caseworker to your place," she says, perched on the edge of her desk. "The worker says your patient disappeared,"

"Jonah, yes," I say. "He's gone. I'm sorry I didn't tell you. I'm sorry I wasted your time. I'm sorry for everything. I'm sorry, sorry, sorry, sorry—"

"Whoa, girl, whoa!" Nurse Viser laughs a mama-laugh and puts her hands on my shoulders. "Forget being sorry. That's not why you're here. How can I help you?"

"I have a friend who has a friend who may have the AIDS virus," I blurt out. I tell her Esther's story without saying her name. "If my friend's friend has the virus, should my friend and her brother and sister wear rubber gloves around her?"

"Not if she's all patched up."

"Good. My friend wanted to make sure her brother and sister were safe."

"They're safe," Nurse Viser says. "HIV/AIDS only spreads through blood, semen, and fecal matter. But you already know that, don't you?" She fixes me with a firm gaze. "What's the real reason you're here?"

I stare at the linoleum, thinking about Isaac Pheto. Nurse Viser watches me for what seems like forever. Finally I take a deep breath. I say: "I have another friend. She was raped when she was a girl, but she's still healthy. The man who raped her is still healthy, too. So she's all right, isn't she? She doesn't have AIDS, does she?"

Nurse Viser puts down her clipboard. "I don't know," she says. "The virus can hide in the body for years."

I suck in a cry. Nurse Viser takes my hand. The alphabet runs through my head as she says—"Would your friend like to be tested?"

"No," I whisper. "She's too scared."

"I understand," she whispers back. "Taking the test *is* scary. But living in fear is worse. At least if your friend takes the test, she'll *know*."

That's the problem," I say. "If she tests positive, she'll know she's going to die."

"Maybe not. Each year new drugs are discovered. People live longer."

"In the West." I bite my lip. "My friend can't afford those drugs. Nobody can."

"In Botswana they have a national drug program. We'll get one too, one day."

"You don't know that."

"You're right," she says, "I don't know it. But I believe it. There's some things you have to believe, Chanda. It's the only way to keep going." She holds my head in her hands like Mama used to do. "In the meantime, if your friend tests positive, she can put her name in a lottery for experimental drug trials. Or on a list to get treatment from a relief agency."

"In a lottery—on a list—that's not enough."

"It's better than nothing."

"But my friend... my friend..." My voice chokes. "You know I'm not talking about a friend, don't you? You know I'm talking about me."

She nods.

All of a sudden tears are pouring down my cheeks. I'm crying. In public. I've let Mama down, but I can't stop. Nurse Viser hands me a tissue. I wipe my eyes. "Please don't tell anybody."

"You're my patient. This is between us." Nurse Viser pauses. She tilts her head, choosing her words carefully. "Have you heard about the Thabo Welcome Centre?"

"No." I shake my head hard. "No. No, I haven't." But I have. Who hasn't? The Thabo Welcome Centre is down the side road from the Section Ten Community Clinic. It's run by Banyana Kaone, this weird old woman everybody calls the AIDS Lady. There's always stories in the papers about her handing out condoms in supermarkets and parks. "The life you save may be your own!" she says. "If you don't care about yourself, care about your partner." She's right. All the same, I keep as far away from the Welcome Centre as I can. If people think you go there, they say you have the sickness.

Nurse Viser raises an eyebrow. "If you take the HIV/AIDS test," she says gently, "let's hope it comes back negative. But if it doesn't, the Welcome Centre is a wonderful place."

I cover my ears. "I don't want to hear this."

"Chanda, if you test positive, you'll need support. The Centre has a counselor ..."

"I don't care. If I have the AIDS virus, I don't want anyone to know. Besides, I can't test positive. I've got too many people to look after."

"Either you have the virus or you don't," Nurse Viser says firmly. "Fear doesn't change the truth."

"Stop it! Stop!" I twist the tissue into a ball and jump to my feet. "I know I should get tested. All right? But I won't! I can't! I just can't!"

I turn and run, tripping over my chair as I race out the door.

31

I BIKE HOME, MY INSIDES IN A KNOT. I tell myself not to think about AIDS or testing. I have to focus on Mrs. Tafa. I have to fight for her phone. I have to fight for Esther. I have to stay calm.

I wheel up to Mrs. Tafa's yard. Soly's making a circle of pebbles around her lawn chair. He jumps up when I come through the gate.

"See my magic circle?" he asks. "I'm doing it just like Mr. Tafa showed me. Whoever sits in the throne gets to make a wish."

"Well, it works," Mrs. Tafa announces. "I was wishing Chanda'd be back so we could have a little talk, and here she is."

"Hooray," Soly bubbles. "Mr. Tafa says my magic circle can protect against evil spirits, too!"

"Maybe you should make one for Chanda," Mrs. Tafa says, giving me a sharp look.

"All right," Soly says. "But I have to finish this one first."

"You do that."

Soly smiles proudly and starts laying more pebbles as Mrs. Tafa hoists herself up and motions me into her house. She shuts the door behind us and whirls on me with the wrath of God. "You should be ashamed of yourself, taking in that Esther Macholo. Don't think I don't know what that tramp's been up to."

"I don't care what you know," I say. "Esther's in trouble. She's my friend."

"You think your mama wants her babies living with a whore?"

"What Esther's done, she's done for her family. Keeping a family together whatever it takes—that's something Mama understands."

"Don't mention your mama and that little bitch in the same breath," Mrs. Tafa thunders. "Esther Macholo can sleep with the pigs, for all I care. But she's not sleeping next door to me. Either you kick her out or I do."

My guts clench. "I'm sorry, Mrs. Tafa. I'm not kicking her out. She's staying right where she is, and there's nothing you can do about it. Now, if you don't mind, I need to use your phone to let Mama know."

Mrs. Tafa hoots. "Nothing I can do about it? As long as that slut's under your roof, you'll never use my phone. You'll never speak to your mama again."

"Oh, yes, I will," I hear myself say. "I'll speak to her one way or another. When I do, I'll—I'll—I'll tell her you made me whore for the money to use a pay phone!"

Mrs. Tafa wobbles backwards. "What?"

"You heard me. I'll tell the whole neighborhood!"

She clutches her chest. "That tramp's under your roof one night, and listen to your filth! It's the devil talking!" She points to her phone. "Go ahead then, Jezebel. Use it, if it means so much to you. Use it and be damned." She runs outside.

I panic: What did I just say? Never mind, I tell myself, it was worth it to see the old goat twitch. I'm shaking as the operator makes the connection to Tiro. The general dealer answers on the fourth ring. There's laughter in the background. I picture a group of men sitting by an old Coca-Cola cooler playing cards and smoking.

"Yeah?" says the dealer with a hearty voice.

"Mr. Kamwendo?"

"That's me."

"It's Chanda Kabelo. Remember me?"

"Yeah. Your granny and grampa are the Thelas. You called a while back when your sister passed."

"Yes, and, well, as you probably know, my mama's visiting Granny and Grampa, and, well, could you please give her a message?"

"Yeah. Sure."

"Tell her everything's going well and we all miss her and to please call, I have to talk to her."

I hear a clunk as if he's put the receiver down on the counter. Then I hear him talking to a customer and a cash register opening. There's the sound of a little bell and a screen door opening and banging shut.

"Hello?" I say. I hear the receiver bounce on the floor and some swearing. "Hello? Are you still there?"

"Yeah, yeah."

"So you got my message?"

"Yeah."

"Tell Mama to make sure to speak to *me*. Not the neighbor lady."

"Sure thing."

I want to ask him if he's seen her, if she's well, if everything's okay. I want to ask him so much. But if I do, maybe he'll wonder why I'm asking. Maybe he'll know something's wrong. Maybe he'll spread things. So I don't ask anything. I just say: "Thank you."

I hang up. An emptiness swallows me. A second ago I was talking to someone only a five-minute walk from Mama. I was that close to her. And now she's hundreds of miles away again.

And I don't know how she is.

And I don't know why she hasn't called.

And I'm afraid to find out.

32

BY LATE AFTERNOON, Esther's swelling is worse. By nighttime, she's unrecognizable. Iris and Soly say hello through the curtain, but she doesn't want anyone but me to see her.

She stays behind the curtain until the middle of the week. I bring her food, but she doesn't eat much even when I spoonfeed it. I leave her a potty and empty it in the outhouse at sunset and daybreak.

Around about Thursday, Esther makes her first steps into the living area. Tiny steps, like an old woman. I hold her by the elbow to keep her from falling down. I also hide the hand mirror by the front door so she won't see what she looks like. It doesn't matter. She can tell by the stares she gets from Soly and Iris.

Back in her room, Esther touches the sides of her head. It hurts her to lift her hands and elbows, but it hurts her even more to imagine what she can't see. "I'm ugly," she weeps. "I wish they'd killed me."

I ignore the last part. "It's just a little swelling," I say. "It'll come down." I hope so. Her head's full of lumps, like a bag stuffed with marula nuts. There's a puckering around the stitches. I pat them clean with a cotton towel and boiled water, but it doesn't make a difference.

Meanwhile, things with Mrs. Tafa are really tense. She keeps babysitting Soly, but she ignores me. The morning after our fight, she stayed out of sight when I lifted him over the hedge.

When I got back at lunch, she was in her lawn chair. I hollered hello. She pretended to be sleeping. I hollered again. She turned her back.

"Mrs. Tafa," I said, "thanks for letting me use your phone yesterday. I'm sorry I was rude."

She got up and walked into her house. Since then we haven't said a word to each other. It's gotten so uncomfortable, I try not to be outside at the same time as her. She'll never forgive me. Not until I get rid of Esther. And I won't do that, ever.

Mealtimes are the worst. Mrs. Tafa manages to get Iris and Soly into her house right beforehand and spoils them with treats. At first they claimed they couldn't hear me calling them. So I started ringing a cowbell. That worked on Soly. Not Iris.

The first time she refused to come, I said, "Soly, is Mrs. Tafa keeping Iris inside her place?"

His little eyes got big as moons. "If I tell, they'll be mad at me."

"Well, if you *don't* tell, *I'll* be mad at you."

"I know. So what am I supposed to do?"

I didn't know what to answer. I just told him to wash his hands and come to the table. Around about the time we were cleaning up, the Little Herself strolled in, eager to let Soly know about the candies he missed.

"Iris," I said, "Mama put me in charge. From now on, you come when I call."

"I'll come when I want," she taunted. "Maybe I won't even come at all."

"Iris—"

She stuck out her tongue, put her hands over her ears and ran around the table yelling at the top of her lungs. I wrestled her to the ground. Sat on her. "You're going to listen to me, Iris."

"Leave me alone. This isn't my real home. You aren't my real sister. I hate you."

I hate you? I thought I was going to die. I went limp. Iris pushed me off and ran outside.

"You should lock her up in her room," said Esther.

"She'd just get out. Then she'd go to Mrs. Tafa. Next thing you know she'd be staying there." I buried my face in my hands. "Why does she hate me?"

"She doesn't hate you."

I want to ask Mrs. Tafa to back me up. But she won't. She wants to be the boss. And she has treats to give. I can't compete.

I can't eat much anymore, either. Or sleep. What if Mama never comes back? What if something happens to her when she does? Will Mrs. Tafa take over? Will she steal my family? How can I stop her?

I wander into the yard in the middle of the night and sit at the side of the house, praying my magic stork will appear. "Please, mma moleane, visit me again. Bring me another dream-vision of Mama." Of course it doesn't. I knew it wouldn't. There's no such thing as magic. The stork I saw was just a stork. It lives by the Kawkee dam. It came here by accident. It'll never come again.

The weekend passes. Mrs. Tafa does the cemetery tour without me. There's still no word from Mama. It's been two weeks since she left. A week since I phoned. Why hasn't she called back?

I want to bang on Mrs. Tafa's door and yell: "Mama's phoned, hasn't she? She wouldn't leave us like this. Not all alone without a word."

But if I bang on her door, what difference would it make? Mrs. Tafa wouldn't tell me. Even if she did, I wouldn't believe her.

I live with this terrible not-knowing into the next week. Then, Tuesday afternoon, something happens. Something so terrible Mama's sure to come home.

33

TUESDAY MORNING I TELL IRIS AND SOLY I'll be late for lunch. "I have to stay at school to do a makeup test for English," I say. "But don't worry. Esther will be here. There's soup left over from last night. She'll give you a bowl."

"Who cares about your soup?" Iris says. "We'll be at Mrs. Tafa's. Mrs. Tafa has figs. Mrs. Tafa has cookies. Mrs. Tafa has everything."

"Iris, I don't have time to argue."

"Good. 'Cause I don't have time to listen." She takes off for school.

I lift Soly over Mrs. Tafa's hedge, and catch up to Iris on my bike. Actually, I don't quite catch up; I stay two blocks behind her. For the past week, she's refused to walk with me. If I don't stay back, she squats on the ground and refuses to budge.

Where's the Iris who loved me? She's gone. I'm a failure.

We near the kindergarten playground. Iris runs into one of

the Sibanda kids and little Lena Gambe. I let her walk the rest of the way with them. There's so much to do before class. I haven't read anything in ages and I have that English test. Mr. Selalame would give me another extension, but I'm too embarrassed to ask. He's been too good to me.

I get to the library before the bell and try to concentrate. I can't. All I can think is: Why is everything such a struggle? Why do I fight with Mrs. Tafa? Maybe it's good that Iris and Soly are getting treats I can't afford. And it's good they get to see so much of Mr. Tafa. Maybe I'm just jealous. Maybe I'm just selfish. Maybe I'm the problem.

The whole morning is like that: My body's in school, but my mind is somewhere else. At lunch, Mr. Selalame sits behind his desk marking while I write the test. Or try to. I stare at the questions like an idiot. My mind is a blank. I write a couple of words, and scribble them out. I fill in the holes in the a's, o's, d's, and p's.

It's no use. My eyes fill. I pull myself to my feet.

Mr. Selalame looks up from his work. "What's the matter?"

"Everything!" I head to the door, bumping into desks.

"Chanda, wait. Talk to me."

I want to! I want to tell him about Mama, Esther, Mrs. Tafa, Iris—how I'm so scared I can't breathe, and I don't know what to do. But all I can say is, "I let you down. I promised to do my work and I can't. I can't do anything."

Before Mr. Selalame can stop me, I'm out the door.

When I get home, Soly's in the front yard. He's blowing bits of chicken down off his hands, watching them float in the air.

"Did you have your soup?" I ask.

He nods.

"And Iris?"

He shakes his head.

I go inside. Esther's at the table. "Have you seen Iris?"

"No," she says. "I think she's at Mrs. Tafa's."

I know I should check, but I can't face Mrs. Tafa. Not to mention Iris with a mouth full of figs. I curl up on my mattress and cover my head with a pillow.

Next thing I know, I hear screaming and crying, a banging at the door. I leap to my feet as Mrs. Tafa barges into the house. She's shaking hysterically. "Chanda, come quick," she cries. "There's been an accident at the junkyard."

There's a huge crowd by the time we arrive. Clusters of neighbors and strangers bunch near the road between the ambulance and the police cars. Some crane their necks for a better look at the action at the rear of the property. Others huddle amongst themselves. I hear bits of things like, "It should never have happened," "Such a tragedy," and "So young, so young."

Mrs. Tafa and I stumble through piles of old tires, paint cans, scraps of barbed wire. The crowd gets thicker the closer we get to the abandoned well. "Out of the way!" Mrs. Tafa yells. "Family coming through." She elbows ahead with one arm while pulling me behind with the other.

Police are keeping people back. They've cordoned the area around the well, stringing rope to a couple of upturned wagons and the rusted hulk of an old car. "Chanda Kabelo, sister of the little girl," Mrs. Tafa says. A policeman lets us under the rope and takes us aside.

"All we know is what we've got from Ezekiel Sibanda and Lena Gambe. You know them?"

I nod. Lena and Ezekiel go to school with Iris. I see Ezekiel close by with his parents. His papa's holding him. His mama's wailing on the ground.

"They're pretty shaken up," the cop continues. "Each time they tell what happened it's a little different. But this is how we've pieced it together." He clears his throat. I brace myself and listen.

It seems that Ezekiel, Lena, and Iris didn't stay at school this morning. Mrs. Ndori was sick. Again. As soon as she took the attendance, she lay down in a corner. Ezekiel, Lena, and Iris took off. This has been happening a lot, the last month.

The three of them came to the junkyard, where they met Ezekiel's little brother Paulo, the one who wears juice cartons for shoes. Ezekiel had sneaked some shake-shake from the family shebeen. Pretty soon they were all drunk.

Iris tottered to the well. She balanced over the lip, calling, "Hello, down there." When the others wanted to know what she was doing, she said her baby sister Sara lived at the bottom. Ezekiel and Lena didn't believe her, but little Paulo did. He said he wanted to see her.

Ezekiel found an old bucket on a chain. Paulo got in. Ezekiel, Lena, and Iris started to lower him down the well. Except the chain wasn't long enough to reach the bottom. They tried to pull him back up, but they didn't have the strength. They called for help. Nobody heard.

Lena panicked and let go. The extra weight was too much for Iris and Ezekiel. The chain slipped. The bucket banged against the stone walls. Paulo fell out. He screamed till he hit the bottom with a thud. The kids called to him, but there was no answer.

Iris said it was all her fault, she was going to climb down

and bring him back up. Ezekiel said she was drunk and stupid and she'd just get herself killed. He and Lena ran off for a grownup. When they returned with the neighborhood, Iris had disappeared.

I see the empty cartons of shake-shake on the ground. I run to the well. No one could survive a drop like that. I don't care. I call down: "Iris? Iris?"

I'm sobbing as Mrs. Tafa starts to pull me away. And then I hear a sound. A whimpering, like in my dream. "Chanda?... Chanda?" But the voice isn't coming from down the well-hole. It's coming from inside an oil bin a stone's throw away. The bin is on its side. Garbage bags spill from its mouth. I watch as the bags are pushed away—as a little body crawls out of its hiding place.

Iris!

Mrs. Tafa kneels down to scoop her up, but Iris runs past her and into my arms. "Chanda, Chanda. I'm sorry. I'll never be bad again. Please don't hate me. Please. I'm so scared."

I hold her tight. "It's okay," I say. "I love you. It's okay."

A fire truck roars up to the junkyard. Three firemen break through the crowd. Their leader rappels down the inside of the well. The other two aim flashlights down to help him see.

There's a pause. Then the fireman calls out: "I've got him. It's a miracle. He's unconscious. But he's alive!"

The crowd cheers as Paulo is raised to the surface. Still, miracles don't just happen. There's a reason Paulo didn't die. Something cushioned his fall. That something is why the fireman throws up. It's why the police tell everyone to move farther away. It's why the firemen return to the well-hole and rappel down again. This time, all three of them.

What they bring back to the light is a nightmare. Something

bent and twisted. Dried out of shape. Draped in rotting cloth. At first, people don't know what it is. But I do.

I'd recognize Jonah's striped bandanna anywhere.

34

Jonah's body is taken to the city morgue.

Iris is fine, except for a little rawness where the chain slid through her hands. After she's checked over, Mrs. Tafa and I get her back home. The whole way, Mrs. Tafa sings hymns of joy, babbles about miracles, and rants that the city of Bonang should fence up all its junkyards. Apparently the two of us are talking again. Lucky me.

I put Iris to bed to sleep off the shake-shake. Then while Esther watches over her and Soly, I go to see Mrs. Tafa. She's already on her lawn chair soothing her nerves with a lemonade.

"I need to call Mama," I say.

"What for?"

"To let her know about Jonah. She'll want to make the arrangements."

Mrs. Tafa sucks the last drops of lemonade up her straw. "That man is no concern of hers. The sonofabitch left, remember? Good riddance, may he rest in peace, or you'd be up to your ears in expenses." I'm about to argue, but Mrs. Tafa doesn't want to fight. She waves me toward the house. "You know where it is."

I thank her, phone Tiro, and tell the general dealer my step-papa's passed. "Can you get my mama to call home right away?"

"Yeah."

Heading home, I ask Mrs. Tafa to holler as soon as there's a ring: "I'll be outside working in the garden."

I till the earth for fresh vegetable rows. I water and weed. Before I know it, it's suppertime. And Mama hasn't called. It doesn't make sense. Jonah is dead. She'd have called if she could. What's wrong? Before I can find out, Auntie Ruth drives up with her boyfriend. He stays in the Corvette listening to the radio while she greets me at the end of the bean rows.

"I'm sorry about your brother," I say.

"Jonah. Yes. Thank you. That's why I'm here. Is your mama around?"

"She's visiting relatives in Tiro."

"Oh." She searches my eyes. "She's well, I hope?"

"Very well, thank you."

"Good." A pause. "Let her know I've claimed the body."

A weight lifts from my heart. "Thank you."

Auntie Ruth's eyes fill. "Jonah did terrible things at the end. But he wasn't a bad man. He just made mistakes, that's all. He didn't mean any harm. He loved your mama."

"Yes. I guess." It doesn't seem right to argue.

"I'm sorry about the wagon. I'm sorry I abandoned him. I'm sorry for everything." Her boyfriend honks the horn. "I have to go. The laying-over is tomorrow. The burial: the day after, seven o'clock, the new cemetery, Phase 6. I didn't want for things to be rushed. It's just, Mr. Bateman gave us a discount."

"That's all right, I'll let Mama know."

"It's not all right. I'm so ashamed. A coffin's been rented for the laying-over, but they're going to bury Jonah in a feedsack."

Her boyfriend honks the horn again.

"I heard you," Auntie Ruth yells. She turns back. "After what he did at our place, the others wanted to leave him at the morgue. I refused. No matter what, I wasn't going to let my baby brother be tossed in the pauper pit. But this, this isn't much better." Her knees give way. I catch her.

"Auntie Ruth, I'll get the money for a coffin. I'll find a way. Don't worry."

"God bless you. God bless you."

Her boyfriend rests his arm on the horn.

"All the best to your mama," she says, scrambling backwards to the Corvette. "I hope she can come. There were good times. I hope people remember the good times." She's into the car. Before she can close the door, it tears off in a cloud of dust.

Mrs. Tafa lets me phone Tiro about the funeral arrangements.

"It's me again," I say to the general dealer. "Chanda Kabelo?"

"Yeah?"

"About my last message, did you get it to Mama?"

"Yeah."

"What did she say?"

"Dunno. Left it with your auntie."

My heart sinks. "Auntie Lizbet?"

"Yeah."

"Well, here's a new message. This time, please give it to Mama personally. Tell her that Auntie Ruth has made the arrangements. Jonah's laying-over's tomorrow night, with the burial right after. She'll have to take the morning bus home or she'll miss everything. Did you get that?"

"Yeah."

"Please, tell her right away?"

"Yeah, yeah."

"Promise?"

"Yeah, yeah."

I hang up. Mrs. Tafa's been pretending to dust the shrine to

Emmanuel on her side table. "Don't get your hopes up," she says.

"What do you mean?"

"Your mama won't be coming."

"How do you know?"

"I just know."

"Well, you're wrong. Mama will be here. If you don't know that, you don't know anything."

Next morning early, I bike to Bateman's to get Jonah a burial coffin. Despite my promise to Auntie Ruth, there's nothing I can afford. Mr. Bateman takes pity. He shows me a pine box that looks like a packing crate. Says he'll sell it to me at half price on account of the bottom boards are warped. "But with the body overtop, no one will know the difference." He agrees to let me pay in instalments: "Your family honors its debts."

Back home, I wait with Iris and Soly for the truck from Tiro. It drives by, but Mama isn't on it. This was her only chance to get here on time. She'll miss Jonah's funeral. Where is she? Why isn't she here? A terrible thought. Maybe she didn't get the message. Maybe I should have called and called until the general dealer got her on the line. Maybe, like always, it's all my fault.

Mrs. Tafa's in her yard. Normally she'd cock her head with a cheery, "What did I tell you?" Today, though, not a single mean word. Why is she being nice? I should be happy. Instead I feel sick to my stomach.

35

AFTER SUPPER, I PACK A CHANGE OF CLOTHES in a knapsack and get ready to leave for the laying-over; Esther will babysit overnight while I'm away. The sun's down; the air is cooling off. I'm pulling on a light jacket when Mrs. Tafa waltzes up to the door. "I thought you might like a ride," she says. "Your Auntie Ruth's is pretty far to be biking at night."

I can't believe my ears. After all the awful things Mrs. Tafa's said about Jonah, she's going to his laying-over? She sees the wonder in my eyes. "Funerals are for the living," she says. "Your Auntie Ruth's a nice woman. She'll appreciate a crowd."

On the way over, Mrs. Tafa tells tales from various laying-overs, some funny, some sad. She remembers Sara's, and laughs at how I got Jonah's sisters to chase down his brothers when they ran off for shake-shakes with Mary. When I don't laugh back, she turns on the radio to the Bible station. A preacher says: "The Lord never gives us more than we can bear." I think of Mama. I think of Esther. I want to smash his face in.

Another twenty minutes and we arrive at Auntie Ruth's. It's in a section like mine: mud huts, two-room prefabs, and cement block homes jumbled up together. Because the funeral's on the cheap, there's no tent for the overnighters. Instead, Auntie Ruth has had her brothers run a tarp along the roof on the right side of her house. One end stretches across to the top of the outhouse, the other end to the top of the shed. It's secured by cement blocks.

A few people drift around, though not any I recognize. They must be friends of Auntie Ruth's. She runs over and introduces Mrs. Tafa and me. "You remember when I babysat Jonah's little ones a few months back?" she tells folks. "Well, this is their big sister, Chanda, and a close friend of the family, Rose Tafa."

Mrs. Tafa discovers an old acquaintance from around the mine. "It's a terrible thing, Jonah's accident," says her friend. "Falling down a well, like that. The poor man never had a chance."

That's what I hear all night: how Jonah's death was an accident. An accident? Were they blind? I want to laugh or scream. But I think of Auntie Ruth and I don't.

Around about midnight Mrs. Tafa's back gives out. She leaves me with a sleeping bag and a promise that she'll return to take me to the burial. True enough, we night guests wake at dawn to the sound of her truck backfiring in from the main road.

Before leaving for the cemetery, we file through Auntie Ruth's to pay our respects to Jonah. The packing crate is closed. Auntie Ruth has wrapped it in a silver polyester sheet that covers the warps and knotholes in the boards.

The service at the cemetery is simple. There's not a huge crowd, but it's big enough not to be embarrassing. I look for Mary. I don't see her. Come to think of it, I haven't seen her in awhile. The coffin is lowered into the ground. There disappears someone else I'll never see again. Life is strange.

I get into Mrs. Tafa's truck and we return to Auntie Ruth's for the burial feast. Auntie had been afraid she'd be shamed for want of food. But last night her brothers gave in and got a leg of beef—and bags of carrots, potatoes, and bread appeared from under her neighbor's shawls. Auntie Ruth is loved.

The ride home is very quiet. For a change, Mrs. Tafa drives under the speed limit. She tries to liven things up, but I just stare out the window. Every so often I feel her itching to read my mind.

"What's the matter?" she says at last.

"Mama should have been here," I say. "She'd have wanted to be."

"You did what you could." Mrs. Tafa reaches into her purse and pulls out a napkin containing a chunk of beef wrapped in bread—a treat she took from the feast. "Besides, there's no reason to think she should have been here. Or would've wanted to be."

"She loved him. He was a papa to Iris and Soly."

"*Was.*" Mrs. Tafa chews deliberately. "He was also a cheating no-account drunk who shamed her and broke her heart. His accident doesn't change a thing."

"'*Accident*'?" I snort under my breath.

"Yes, 'accident,'" Mrs. Tafa says. "What else would you call it?"

"I'd call it suicide or murder."

Mrs. Tafa nearly crashes into the ditch. She brakes and faces me. "What are you talking about?"

"I know there won't be an investigation," I say calmly, "but we both know the truth. Jonah threw himself down that well—or got thrown down that well—because he had AIDS."

"Don't say that. If Jonah had the bug, folks'll be saying your mama has it too."

"I'll bet they already do."

"Did, maybe, once upon a time. But not since I fetched Mrs. Gulubane. Because of her, they say your mama has a bewitchment. And Jonah's had an accident. That's the truth they want to believe. It's the truth you should want to believe too."

"Well, I don't. Mama's in trouble."

"You don't know that."

"Then why hasn't she called?"

"Because."

"Because why?"

"Just because."

"Tell me."

"No."

I take a deep breath and throw open the door of the truck. "Thank you, Mrs. Tafa, I can walk home from here."

"Chanda, there's things you don't understand."

"Maybe. But I understand this. Mama needs me. When I get home, I'm packing my bags. I'm going to Tiro."

"How?" she snorts. "You don't have the money for bus fare."

"I'll hitchhike."

"Are you crazy? A young girl alone on the road? You don't have to be a whore to be raped."

I walk down the road, Mrs. Tafa idling after me. She calls through the open window: "Chanda—what makes you think your mama wants to see you?"

I look straight ahead and keep walking. "Why wouldn't she?" I start to run, but she sticks to me like flypaper.

"Maybe your mama never expected to come home. Maybe she meant her good-bye to be forever."

"You're lying."

"Am I? I made her a promise, Chanda. I can't let you go to Tiro."

"Try and stop me."

36

MY HEAD SWIMS AS I RACE INTO THE FRONT YARD. Mrs. Tafa brakes hard and runs after me. Esther is inside with Soly and Iris. Mouths open, they watch me slam the door, bolt it, press my back against it. Outside, Mrs. Tafa bangs away with her fist, demanding to be let in.

I cover my ears and scream, "Go Away Go Away Go Away Go Away!!!"

Soly cries. Esther holds him. Iris runs into the bedroom and hides under the cover. At last Mrs. Tafa is exhausted. I hear her panting. Then she says, "Fine. Go ahead. Break your mama's heart. Break your own heart while you're at it." Through the slats of the shutters I see her heave her way to the gate. She pauses to wipe her forehead with the back of her arm, then disappears from sight.

I'm bunched up on the floor. Esther and Soly kneel beside me. "It's all right, Chanda," Soly says solemnly. "We love you."

I give him a big hug and a kiss. Then I get him to bed, and tell him and Iris a story. Pretty soon they're cuddled up napping. Or at least I think they're napping. In case their ears are open, I motion Esther out back. We crouch behind the outhouse, and I tell her what happened on the ride home.

"I have to get to Mama. But what'll I do about Iris and Soly?"

"Don't worry," Esther says. "I'll take care of them. After what happened at the junkyard, Iris won't be going far. And if worst comes to worst, well, there's Mrs. Tafa. Even if she's mad at you, she won't let anything happen to them."

I nod. "Then I better pack. It's almost noon. If I'm going to hitchhike, I want as much light as possible."

"Don't hitchhike," Esther says. "It isn't safe."

"I haven't got a choice."

"Yes, you do." She pats my hand. "Wait here."

Esther gets up and goes inside. A minute later she comes back carrying an old cardboard shoebox tied up with string. She sits beside me and opens it carefully, as if it's the most precious thing in the world. It is. Under several copies of her parents' funeral programs, and their obituary clippings from the local newspaper, are two envelopes stuffed with savings.

"There's ninety-eight dollars, plus some money from here," she says. "Auntie used to come into my shed and steal. I caught her a few times. Once she said she was only taking what was hers for looking after me. Another time, she said she was taking it for God, so I wouldn't go to hell. Anyway, I used to leave some around where she'd find it, and hid the rest in this box. It was money to bring my brothers and sister back together. But it's not enough. It'll never be enough. Better you should have it."

I look at the money—more than enough to get me to Tiro and bring Mama home. Then I look at the scars on Esther's face.

"I'm sorry," I say. "I can't take this."

Esther seems to shrink. "Why? Because it's whore money?"

I open my mouth, but nothing comes out.

"You saved my life," Esther continues. "If you hadn't taken me in, I'd be dead. I need to say thank you. Please let me."

And I do. I take the money, and I pack, and I get on the truck to Tiro. I don't call ahead. I don't give anyone the chance to say, "Don't come." I just get on the truck and wave good-bye. "Don't worry," I call out, watching my little ones disappear in Esther's arms. "I'll be back soon. I'll be back with Mama."

Is it a sin I took the money? Is it a sin I'm on this truck? I don't know. Even worse, I don't care. I don't have time to worry about right and wrong. All I have time to worry about is Mama.

We pass through hours of country. Here and there a village. The sun sets. Headlights pick up jungle, abandoned huts, an elephant, a few cleared lots. I think about what Mrs. Tafa said. That Mama never expected to come home. That her good-bye was meant to be forever. Mrs. Tafa is Mama's best friend. Did Mama tell her a secret?

I knew she was sick with AIDS. But I'd tried not to think about how sick. Now, as the truck rattles through the night, it comes to me clear as day. Mama is more than sick. Mama is dying. Maybe she's already dead.

I whisper the words aloud. I whisper them as if they're a secret—a secret I've been keeping even from myself. I begin to perspire, but I don't cry. My mind is too full: Mama hates Tiro. She said we'd never live there. So why did she go there to die? Why not stay home, with me and Soly and Iris? Was it the AIDS? Did she think we'd be ashamed? That we wouldn't love her anymore?

"Mama," I whisper, "please hear me. If you're still alive, I make you a promise. You're not going to die in Tiro. I'm going to bring you home. I love you. We all do. Always. No matter what."

It's eleven o'clock. We leave the highway. Soon we're at the edge of the village. We pull up to the general dealer's. On the left, there's a gas tank; on the right, a handful of men sitting around smoking cigarettes and drinking. A single bare light bulb hangs above the door. A neon beer sign flickers in the window.

In a few minutes I'll see Mama. Or know what's happened to her.

Dear God, if you're out there, please help me.

We rumble to a halt, the air thick with shadows. Alive with questions.

PART FOUR

37

I TRY TO BE CALM. If I'm to help Mama, I'll need a clear head.

I stand up on the flatbed and look around. The general dealer's is a lot like I remember: its stuccoed walls are chipped and in need of a whitewash. The fluorescents and neon sign are new, though. So are the pockets of light spreading out from behind the store into the distance—firepits planted along streets and in front yards and neighborhoods that didn't exist when Papa was alive.

We came back to Tiro once a year then. We'd get off the truck like I'm doing now and one of my papa-uncles with a buggy would take us to the cattle post. It was fun to play with my cousins again. And to see my older sister Lily—the one who'd stayed behind to marry her boyfriend down the road.

During our visits, we'd find time to trek to Mama's family post too. I was afraid of my Granny and Grampa Thela. Their arms were always folded and they never smiled. Mama was very particular about how my brothers and I were dressed and how we behaved when we'd visit. We had to be perfect.

My brothers were lucky; they got to go off hunting with my uncles. But me, I had to stay with Mama and my aunties. Granny and Grampa Thela would take us over to Auntie Amanthe's burial stone, where Auntie Lizbet would hobble around serving tea, biscuits, and hard looks. No matter how hungry I was, I tried not to eat. Any crumb that stuck to my lip or fell on my dress got a sharp word.

After Papa and my brothers died, Mama and I only came back to Tiro once. That last time was when Iris was a baby, and Mama was pregnant with Soly. I'm sure Papa's family didn't expect her to stay single forever. But seeing her with another man's child, and pregnant with the child of yet another... well. Mama's marriage to Papa had cost them dearly. These "other men" in her life gave them an excuse to cut us off.

As for Granny and Grampa Thela, they didn't miss us. Mama sent them letters in care of my older sister Lily. Lily read them to Granny and Grampa, and wrote a few words back on their behalf. That's how we found out they'd moved from the cattle post to the village. Tiro had finally gotten electricity, along with standpipes and a health clinic.

My granny, my aunties, and female cousins moved first; my grampa, uncles, and older male cousins joined them on weekends, leaving the cattle to hired herd boys. But the men couldn't stand their own cooking, so in the end they moved to town, too. Each morning before dawn they'd go to the post by cart and bicycle. They still do, along with men from other posts who've made the move.

On the ground now, I drop my bag and stretch. The general dealer ambles over from the circle of drinkers and starts to unload the crates of dry goods that came with me from Bonang. He looks like I remember, only shorter.

"Mr. Kamwendo?"

He squints at me in the dim spill of light from the store. "Yeah?"

"It's me. Chanda Kabelo?"

"My Lord!" He wipes his hands on his work pants. We shake. He's not drunk, but I smell the alcohol on his breath. "You're all grown up. Last time I saw you, you were knee-high to a cricket. Sorry to hear about your step-papa."

"Thank you."

"So what brings you to Tiro? Visiting your Granny and Grampa Thela?"

"Not exactly. I've come to see Mama."

He looks puzzled.

"You know... Mama? She's with my granny and grampa? I called two days ago? I asked you to pass on messages?" Something in the way he scratches his head makes me nervous. "What's wrong?"

"Nothing," he says. "Only your Mama isn't here anymore."

"What?"

"She's not here. She's gone."

38

MAMA'S GONE. But she isn't dead. That's what I keep telling myself as Mr. Kamwendo walks me to my Granny and Grampa Thela's.

"I took your messages over," he says, pointing out the potholes with his flashlight. "I asked for your mama like you told me, but your Auntie Lizbet said she'd already left. Said she caught a ride from some friend at the post. Your granny dropped by the store later. Phoned a message to your neighbor lady. You didn't get it?"

"No," I say.

"And your mama never showed up?"

I shake my head.

"Strange." He frowns. "Oh, well, I'm sure there's an explanation."

"I'm sure there is too," I say, and curse Mrs. Tafa in my heart. "When Mama was here... did you see her much?"

"Can't say as I did. Not surprising, with all the folks she had to visit. Saw her when she arrived, though."

"How was she?"

"Travel sick. It's a long trip. Why?"

"Just wondering."

Tiro's laid out in a broad grid, lots of space between clusters of huts. We cross a dozen streets. A few more and we're at the village edge. Behind us, the firepits are dying out. Their coals burn like orange eyes in the night.

The general dealer pauses. "Your granny and grampa's compound is over there," he says, pointing his flashlight into the darkness. "It's faster if we cut through this field."

I can't see a thing. The flashlight's batteries are running low. I hesitate. "Are you sure?"

"Yeah, yeah. It's pretty much cleared. Just a few weeds."

I take a deep breath and follow him into the pitch black. The flashlight flickers like a firefly. We walk in silence.

"I'm s'prised no one showed up to meet you," he says at last.

"I didn't tell them I was coming."

"Oh." A pause. "So no one's expecting you?"

"No."

More silence. I wish I knew what he was thinking. My throat's a little dry. "Are we nearly there?" I ask.

"Oh, yeah."

The field is bigger than I imagined when we started walking. I look over my shoulder. The road's disappeared. So has the village. All I can see are the pale tufts of grass lit by the wavering flashlight.

"How much further?"

"Just a piece."

The hairs on the back of my neck begin to prickle. I'm tempted to turn and run, but I'm scared. Who knows what's out there. Or what's ahead. "Maybe we should go back to the street."

"I know where I'm going."

"Are you sure?"

"Yeah, yeah." He chuckles quietly.

This walk was a bad idea. I should have phoned before I left home. I should have had an uncle waiting with a buggy. I should have told the dealer I was expected. I should have—

Suddenly the flashlight goes out. The general dealer grabs my arm. He pulls me back. I try to scream, but I can't. He whaps the flashlight on the side of his leg. The light snaps back on.

"Careful about those bushes," he says. Not two steps ahead of me is a thicket of jackalberries. "You don't want to rip yourself up on those thorns."

"Thank you," I say as he lets go of my arm.

The moon comes out from behind a cloud. Straight ahead, a small circle of mud huts is silhouetted against the sky.

"We're here," Mr. Kamwendo says. "Your aunties, uncles, and cousins live in the side huts, except for your Auntie Lizbet. She stays in the center one with your granny and grampa." He walks me to the main door and knocks.

"Ko ko," he calls out, so they won't be scared by our midnight visit. "It's me, Sam Kamwendo. I've brought you a surprise guest."

Inside, somebody lights a lamp. The light glows through slits in the shutters.

"A guest?" It's an old woman's voice. A voice I barely remember.

"Granny? It's me. Chanda."

Confusion. "Lizbet, get the door."

Muttering. A curse. The bolt is pulled back, the door opened. Auntie Lizbet peers suspiciously from the gloom. "What are you doing here?"

"I've come to see Mama."

"She's gone."

"That's what I told her," says the general dealer.

Auntie Lizbet spares him a nod. "Evening, Sam."

"I phoned two days ago," I say. "Mr. Kamwendo says that's when you said she'd left. But she hasn't come home. Where is she?"

Granny Thela shuffles up, bundled in a housecoat, skin as cracked as a dried mud hole. "She's with friends in Henrytown. Her ride broke down. Radiator trouble. She'll be home when it's fixed. Maybe a week."

"Where did you hear that from? Who told you?" I turn to the general dealer. "Did Mama phone from Henrytown?"

"Are you calling your granny a liar?" Auntie Lizbet snaps. Aunties and uncles appear at the doors of the other huts.

Mr. Kamwendo clears his throat. "I think it's time for me to go."

"'Night," Granny Thela says sharply. "Thanks for your trouble. No need to worry about Lilian. Everything's fine."

"Whatever you say, Mrs. Thela." The dealer tips his hat, turns, and ambles back across the field.

Granny waves her chin at my aunties and uncles. "It's nothing. Just Lilian's girl. We can handle it."

"Get inside," Auntie Lizbet orders me. While Granny bars the door, Auntie Lizbet grabs my arm, yanks me to the kitchen table, and pushes me onto a stool. I hop up. She shoves me down again. I bounce back, this time fists clenched. She raises her cane.

"What's going on?" comes a frail voice from behind a curtain.

"It's nothing, Papa," Auntie Lizbet shouts. "Go back to sleep."

"I hope you're satisfied," Granny Thela hisses, "waking your grampa, and him a sick old man with bad bones, deaf in the bargain."

"Where's Mama?"

"We told you. Henrytown."

"Give me the address. A phone number."

"Go back to Bonang," Auntie Lizbet says. "She'll be there soon enough."

"I don't believe you. Tomorrow morning I'm going to the police."

"A troublemaker, just like your mama," Granny Thela says.

Auntie Lizbet waves the Bible from the kitchen table. "Remember the ten commandments, girl. 'Honor thy father and thy mother that thy days may be long upon the land which the Lord thy God giveth thee.' Your mama got what was coming to her. So will you."

I freeze. "Is she dead?"

"She defied God, her ancestors, dishonored her family, coveted another, committed adultery—"

"*Is she dead??*"

"She has the disease. God's curse."

"Disease isn't God's curse," I say, "any more than your club foot. What sin did you get that for?"

Auntie Lizbet swings her cane at my head. "God's vengeance!"

I duck just in time. "You wouldn't know God if he bit you on the nose!"

Auntie Lizbet roars and swings again. I roll under the table for protection. The cane hits the hard boards, sending tin cups flying.

"Lizbet!" Granny Thela barks. "Enough! Enough!"

Auntie Lizbet lowers her cane slowly. She backs up. I crawl out from under the table. Granny Thela sinks into her rocker and motions me to sit in the chair opposite her. I do.

We stare at each other for a long time. Maybe it's the smoke of the oil lamp, but her eyes are damp. In her face I see Mama, and a little of myself. Does she see the same in me?

"We kept your mama here as long as we could," she says. "We built a lean-to behind the woodpile. But she took a turn for the worse. Her legs gave out. A week ago she lost control of her bowels. We fed her tea and bark from the baobab. It didn't work. We had to hide her someplace else. Someplace far away where the stench of the sickness wouldn't shame the family."

"She's always shamed the family," whispers Auntie Lizbet. "Even in dying."

Before, I might have smacked Auntie Lizbet across the face. Not now. Now, I'm too empty even to be angry. "Where is she?"

"At the cattle post," Granny says. "In one of the old huts."

I grip the arms of my chair. "What?"

"We're doing what we can. We've given your mama a mat and a blanket. Each day one of us brings fresh food and water."

"Who's with her now?"

Granny pauses. "Nobody."

"Nobody? My mama's alone in the bush?"

Granny's face fills with despair. "We can't stay with her. If we did, folks would know something's wrong."

"Besides," Auntie Lizbet interrupts, "it makes no difference to your mama. Her mind is gone. She can't move. She won't eat. She barely drinks. She doesn't even know us anymore."

I look to Granny. Tears roll down her cheeks. "I'm sorry, Chanda," she says. "This is a small village. We didn't know what else to do."

39

AT FIRST LIGHT, I START FOR THE CATTLE POST. The air is crisp. Fruit bats swoop around me, flying home to rest till nightfall.

I leave Tiro and head for the highway. From there I travel north to the giant baobab. A family of baboons chatters at me from the upper branches. They toss twigs as I pass, moving off the paved road onto a dirt trail that winds into the bush.

There are no fences marking the borders of the posts. I know whose family belongs where by the rocks, the hillocks, the bushes and trees. The younger trees have grown since I was here last, a few are missing. It doesn't matter. It's like when I bike through downtown Bonang and notice a new store, or a streetseller missing from the bazaar; despite the changes, I know exactly where I am and where I'm going.

A few miles in, I come to the three boulders at the east corner of Mama's family post. A lizard suns itself on the largest, mouth open for bugs. I head off the road and into a maze of cattle paths. Geckos skitter from my shadow.

Granny's told me where I'll find Mama: in an abandoned hut out by Auntie Amanthe's burial stone. When Auntie Amanthe died, the Malungas returned her body and her stillborn, I guess on account of "Mama's curse." Granny and Grampa buried them at the family compound. The spirit doctor said the evil lived on. He said they should leave the compound and build another, or it would kill their cattle. So they did, moving to where the herd boys stay now.

After a hard walk, I near Mama's hut. I remember it from the times Granny took Mama and me to Auntie Amanthe's stone. Even then, the thatched roof was collapsed and the mud walls were crumbling. Now all that's left is a partial clay curve and the ring of exposed mopane poles. Half these stakes have fallen to the ground; the others are held in place by termite mounds. Weeds fill what used to be the inside rooms.

I pause. "Mama?"

Everything's still, except for a circle of large black birds hovering overhead. I continue to walk toward the hut, barely daring to breathe. But soon I'm not walking. I'm running as fast as I can. "Mama? Mama?"

A couple of poles have been propped against the clay curve. They're loosely covered with scrap thatching. On the ground, in the shadows under the thatching, I see a water jug, an untouched plate of food, and a mat. And lying on the mat, I see a small still bundle draped in a stained sheet buzzing with flies. I kneel down under the thatching and crawl beside it. I touch its thin shoulder.

"Amanthe?" comes a voice as quiet as breath. "Is that you, Amanthe?"

"No, Mama," I whisper. "It's Chanda."

For a moment, nothing. Then the bundle curls in on itself. "Forgive me, Amanthe."

"No, Mama. Auntie Amanthe is dead. It's me. Chanda."

She shudders. "Chanda?"

"Yes."

I draw back the sheet. Mama rolls her head toward me. Her eyes are confused and frightened. "Chanda?"

"It's all right, Mama. I'm here." I take my handkerchief and soak a little water from the bottom of the jug. I pat her forehead, wet her lips.

Mama's eyes cloud. "Chanda, I'm lost."

"It's all right. I've found you." I hold her hand. "We're going home."

40

I HAVEN'T COME TO THE POST BY MYSELF. Before leaving Tiro, I stopped at the health clinic, where I explained my story. A nurse and a helper rode out with me in the clinic van. I gave them directions as we drove along the trail till we reached the entrance to the post. Then they parked the van and followed me into the bush on foot. As soon as we reached the compound, they began searching the outlying ruins while I headed to the hut. Now, as I signal that Mama's been found, they hurry over with a stretcher.

The nurse opens her medical kit and pulls out an intravenous bag filled with fluids, antibiotic, and painkiller. She inserts a tube into the bag; the other end of the tube she sticks into a vein in Mama's arm. Very carefully she and the helper lift Mama onto the stretcher. With the helper taking one end, and the nurse and me the other, we make our way back to the van.

A few minutes later, we're at the clinic. Mama is carried through an open waiting area to the examining room. The doctor checks Mama over and asks me questions. I tell him about her headaches, her night sweats, her diarrhea.

He frowns. "I think she should have an HIV/AIDS test."

Mama's too lost to give consent. It's up to me. I swallow hard. "Go ahead." It's not like I don't already know the results.

"There aren't any hospital beds available," the doctor says, as he draws the blood. "Your mama will have to be cared for at home."

"Home is in Bonang. There's no way she'll survive on a flatbed."

The doctor pauses. "We don't get much call for the van," he says slowly. "I bike to house calls. In a pinch, my brother has a Jeep. Tell you what: Pay for the gas there and back, and I'll have the helper drive you."

"Thank you." I squeeze Esther's money pouch under my dress. "Could I also buy some painkillers?"

He nods. "There's already some in the drip bag, but I can sell you more in case she needs it." He shows me how to change the drip and catheter bags. "I'll arrange for Bonang General to send you a caseworker." I can tell he thinks Mama won't be alive long enough for it to matter.

Before we leave, I ask to call ahead. There's only one phone; it's on a desk in the reception area. I turn my back on the patients lining the walls, so I can pretend nobody can hear me.

"How-de-ya-do?" The voice on the other end is unmistakable.
"Mrs. Tafa?"

At the sound of my voice, Mrs. Tafa gasps so loud she nearly sucks the phone down her throat. "Where are you calling from?"

"The clinic in Tiro. I'm with Mama."

"Lord Almighty!"

"Tell Esther to get Soly and Iris cleaned up. We're coming home."

"You're bringing your mama here?"

"Yes."

"No!" Mrs. Tafa shrieks. "Your granny phoned this morning from the general dealer. She told me everything. If they couldn't hide the disease in Tiro, you won't be able to hide it here."

"So what?"

"So *what?* The neighbors will know."

"I don't care," I say. "If Mama's going to die, she's going to die at home, surrounded by family who love her."

"Chanda, listen to me, girl—"

"No. You listen to me, Mrs. Tafa," I shout. "I'm tired of lies and hiding and being afraid. I'm not ashamed of AIDS! I'm ashamed of being ashamed!"

I slam the phone down. When I turn around I see walls of open mouths. All around the room, patients and their families have turned to see who said the unsayable.

I put my hands on my hips. "What are you looking at?"

They run from the clinic as if they're on fire.

On the drive back, Mama lies on a cot in the rear of the van, attached to her IV drip and a catheter. I sit beside her, holding her hand and placing cold compresses on her forehead. She doesn't know where she is, who I am, or what's happening.

She tries to sit up, and cries out, "Amanthe, don't marry Tuelo. There'll be bad luck. I know things, Amanthe." Then her head falls back on her pillow, her eyes roll into her head, and her lips flutter soundlessly.

When I think she's asleep, I pour out my heart. I tell her about Esther, how she's been living at our place, how she gave me the money to come here, money she was saving so her brothers and sister could be together. "I want to ask her brothers and sister to live with us, Mama."

For a moment, Mama opens her eyes. Her eyes are clear. She nods. Did she understand? I don't know. Her eyes cloud again, her mind wanders off, and soon she's whispering to Papa and Auntie Amanthe, or sleeping, or singing bits of song to Sara.

41

IT'S LATE AFTERNOON BY THE TIME WE GET HOME. Soly and Iris are waiting with Esther at the side of the road.

They're not alone. Neighbors dot the front yards along the street. They pretend to garden, to simmer seswa on their firepits, or to chat across their hedges; but they have an eye out, curious about who or what "those kids and the hooker-girl" are waiting for.

When the van stops by our gate, they begin to drift over. They stare at the rubber gloves on the clinic helper. They stare at the tubing and the IV drip bag attached to Mama as he slides her from the rear of the van onto a stretcher-trolley.

The one neighbor missing is the one neighbor who knew we

were coming. Mrs. Tafa. I picture her hiding behind her shutters, afraid of living next door to an AIDS family.

Soly and Iris run up to me. I hug them. "Mama's very sick."

"Is she going to get better?"

"We can hope."

Holding hands, they follow the helper and me into the house and on to Mama's room. There's a homemade frame with baby pictures of us kids hanging above her bed. I take it down and we use the nail to hang up the IV bag. We lift Mama from the trolley onto her mattress, and pull up her cover.

Iris, Soly, and I each give her a kiss on the forehead. Mama's unconscious, but she seems to know what's happening. A smile crosses her lips and for a moment the lines around her eyes and forehead soften.

"You rest now, Mama," I whisper.

I walk the helper back to the van. I pretend not to notice that the neighbors haven't budged. The helper hops into the van and starts the engine, then hands me a box of rubber gloves through the window. He edges the van through the crowd and is gone.

Everyone's staring. I want to close my eyes and make the world disappear. I want to recite the alphabet until my brain melts. But I don't. I force a smile. "Thank you for coming," I say.

Silence.

I know each of these people—I've known them since we moved here. They're good people, fine people. But they look at me like I don't exist. A million terrible thoughts fill my head. Are we without friends from this moment on? Cut off? Shunned? Left to live and die alone?

It's now that a miracle happens. A screen door bangs shut on the other side of the hedge. All eyes turn. Striding toward me, twirling her floral umbrella, comes Mrs. Tafa. She marches up as bright as a sunrise and kisses me on both cheeks.

"Welcome home," she says. She nods to the crowd. "I don't know what the rest of you folks are doing here, but I've come to say hello to my good friend Lilian."

The crowd blinks.

"Is something the matter?" Mrs. Tafa demands.

There's a low rumble.

Mrs. Tafa arches an eyebrow. "I know what goes on behind each of your doors," she says, sizing them up one by one. "This is the best family on the block. If any of you disagree, I'll be happy to share your secrets."

Some nervous coughs. A few wives give their husbands the evil eye. Young men look down, toe the dirt. And from all around, voices begin to break the silence.

"Glad to see you back," says old Mr. Nylo the ragpicker.

"You're in our prayers," say the Lesoles.

Under the watchful eye of Mrs. Tafa, they each come up to give their regards or shake my hand. As soon as they leave, some of the shakers wipe their hands on their pants and dresses. It doesn't matter. The Keeper of Scandals has spoken. The curse has been broken.

42

WHEN MRS. TAFA AND I ENTER THE HOUSE, Esther whisks Soly and Iris to their room. I close the front door and Mrs. Tafa starts shaking. She looks out the window to make sure everyone's truly gone. Then she clutches her hand to her chest and collapses in a chair at the kitchen table. "Water! Water!"

I bring her a glass. She gulps it down and has another.

"Mrs. Tafa," I say, "thank you for what you did out there."

She gives me a wave of her hankie as if it was nothing. "Is it all right if I see your mama?"

I nearly fall on the floor. It's the first time I've ever heard Mrs. Tafa ask permission for anything. "Come," I say, and take her into Mama's room. We sit together by the side of the bed. As I watch her watching Mama, she doesn't seem so fierce anymore. Instead she seems like I feel: scared and alone.

"Chanda," she says at last, "forgive me. Your mama and me, we thought we knew best. We thought if the traditional doctor came, your mama would have an excuse to disappear, to pass in secret. Your mama thought she'd spare you shame. Me, I just thought about myself. People knew we were friends. To have her die here... like this... after everything I'd said about the sickness... I was afraid."

"It's all right," I say.

The minute I say it's all right, Mrs. Tafa buries her head between her knees and wails. I put my arm around her shoulder. She grabs hold of me and blubbers like a baby.

"You thanked me for what I did out there," she weeps. "It's not me you should thank. It's my son. My Emmanuel."

But Emmanuel's dead, I think.

"When you called from the hospital," Mrs. Tafa continues, "I was so terrified. I closed the shutters and hid behind the closet curtain. When the van drove up, I peeked between the shutter slats. I saw the neighbors coming. I went back to hide, to leave you to face them alone. That's when I saw the shrine to my Emmanuel sitting on the side table. His baptismal certificate, funeral program, envelope of baby hair, and in the middle of it all, his photograph. His eyes called to me from the grave, 'Mama, for my sake, you know what to do.' He was right. I knew. And this time I didn't betray him."

"But you've never betrayed him."

"Oh, yes, I have. Ever since he died." She wrings her hankie. "When Emmanuel won his scholarship to study law in Jo'burg, we were all so proud. He'd never been one to waste his time on girls. Only on books. Now his studies had paid off. I remember the last time we spoke. He was at a phone booth on his way to his doctor to take the physical for his travel documents."

"Just before his hunting accident, right?"

She shakes her head. "My boy didn't hunt. There was no accident. He shot himself."

My head swims. "What?"

"As part of the physical, his doctor gave him an AIDS test. The test came back positive. Emmanuel borrowed a rifle from a friend. He went into the bush, put the rifle in his mouth and blew his head off. You see, he didn't know how to tell us, my husband and me. He was afraid we wouldn't understand. He was afraid we wouldn't love him anymore."

"But that's crazy."

"Is it?" She wipes her eyes. "Then why have we dishonored his death with a lie?"

We sit very still.

"I won't tell anyone," I whisper.

"It's all right if you do," she says. "Seeing how you've stood by your mama, well, it's how I want to stand by my Emmanuel. Facing the neighbors today, I've never felt so tall. I hope my boy was watching."

Before Mrs. Tafa goes, she takes my mama's hand and whispers in her ear: "Oh Lilian, you have such a daughter. Such a daughter."

43

TWO DAYS LATER, MAMA SLIPS INTO A COMA.

Esther looks after Iris and Soly, while Mrs. Tafa organizes different neighbors to bring food and help with chores. I stay with Mama the whole time, changing her, and turning her over to keep away bedsores. At night I pass out on a mat beside her. I'm glad I don't have time to think. If I did, I'd go crazy.

In the middle of the week, I get a visitor. Mr. Selalame. Without thinking, I throw myself into his arms. "Oh, Mr. Selalame, I'm frightened."

When I settle down, I have Esther sit with Mama, and Mr. Selalame and I go for a walk. We end up at the park around the block, sitting on the swings.

"I'm sorry about school," I say. "I'm sorry for letting you down."

"You didn't."

I wipe my eyes. "I don't think I can go back. When this is over, I'll have to work."

"I know." He pauses. "Chanda, this isn't the right time to make decisions. But I want you to know I've made enquiries. A lot of teachers are sick. There aren't enough qualified replacements. You were one of my best students. I've recommended you at the elementary school. When you're ready—if you're interested—the principal says you can have a job as a supply."

I know this is wonderful news. Working supply will help us get by—and I can keep an eye on Iris—Soly too, he'll be starting school next year. All the same, I think of my dreams. How I wanted to graduate. Get a scholarship. Be a lawyer. A doctor. A full teacher. My dreams are over. I choke up.

Mr. Selalame knows why I'm crying. He puts a hand on my shoulder. "Chanda, you keep your dreams alive, you hear? This is only for now. Dreams are for your whole life."

At night I sit with Mama after everyone's asleep. I hold her hand and tell her what Mr. Selalame said. "It's not perfect," I say quietly, "but there's always the future. And meanwhile, Soly and Iris and I will be all right. We'll survive."

They tell me Mama can't hear me. All the same, when I say my news, her body relaxes. She begins to rest easy.

She stays with us for one last day. Iris and Soly know what's coming. They sit beside her and tell her stories. I say that even though Mama's sleeping, deep inside she knows they're there.

Every so often, one of them cries. I try not to show how afraid I am. "It's all right," I say. "I'll be with you."

"But we want Mama. We don't want her to go."

"She won't be gone. Not really. Whenever you miss her, just close your eyes. She'll be as close as your nearest thought." I hope that's true. Even if it isn't, I don't know what else to say.

People think I'm imagining things when I tell them this, but I don't care. It's what I know:

The end came in the middle of the night. I was on my mat next to Mama. Soly and Iris were in the other room with Esther. For some reason I woke up. Mama was looking at me.

I raised myself on an elbow. Mama's in a coma, I thought. Am I dreaming?

"Don't worry," she said. "You're awake. I've just come back to say good-bye."

"No," I pleaded. "Not yet. Please, not yet."

"You'll do fine," she laughed gently. "I believe in you."

And she passed.

I went to get Iris and Soly. At the door to their room, I saw them standing at the window with Esther.

"They just woke up," Esther whispered.

I was about to tell them about Mama when Iris called out, "Chanda, come quick." She was pointing at something outside.

I hurried over. There, perched on the wheelbarrow, was my stork. It craned its neck toward us. Iris and Soly waved. The stork raised its right foot as if giving us a blessing. Then it arched its back and began to fly, circling the yard three times before disappearing into the night.

I held my babies close.

"That was Mama, wasn't it?" whispered Soly.

My mind said no, but my heart said, "Yes."

"She's gone now?"

"Yes."

IT HASN'T BEEN EASY SINCE MAMA DIED. Some days I'm so tired I can barely move, and the pain of Mama's death is so big I don't know where to put it. I try to keep busy, like she did.

The Tafas looked after the funeral expenses, including a moriti.

"I'll pay you back," I said.

"No," Mrs. Tafa insisted. "We're paying *you* back."

The whole community came to the burial feast. For once, nobody had to lie about the cause of death. We could breathe freely.

Every so often someone came up and whispered: "I have a parent who's sick." Or a grandparent. Or an aunt, an uncle, a cousin, a best friend. "You're the first person we've been able to tell."

Before Mama left for Tiro, she'd written a will. One copy was left with Mrs. Tafa, a second with the priest. Mama gave everything—the house and her belongings—to me in trust. I was put in charge of Iris and Soly.

I asked Esther to move in permanently and to bring her brothers and sister along. One brother was happily settled with her Uncle Kagiso, but the other brother and sister came. The house was crowded for awhile, but Mr. Tafa built a pair of extra rooms at the side.

We've also increased the size of our chicken coop and vegetable garden. Weekends, we all chip in on the chores. Weekdays, most of the housework is done by Esther while I do supply work at the elementary school.

The hardest time was when I took Soly and Iris to the hospital to see Nurse Viser. Esther came, too, with her brother and sister.

"Awhile ago, you asked if I wanted to be tested for AIDS," I said. "I wasn't ready then. I am now. This is my family. We all want the truth."

The tests came back negative. Except for Esther's. We held each other and cried.

Nurse Viser put Esther on a list to get anti-retroviral drugs through a relief agency. "The bad news is, the list is long and it'll take awhile for your name to get to the top," she said. "The good news is, your health is excellent and you may be able to get treatment before you're sick. Remember, new drugs are discovered each year. Don't give up hope."

Nurse Viser also arranged for Esther to meet with the counselor at the Thabo Welcome Centre. Esther carries on as if she's fearless. But it's only an act. The day of her appointment she was terrified.

"Would you like me to go with you?" I asked.

"Are you sure?" she hesitated. "People may think you have AIDS too."

"So what? I don't care what people think anymore."

Esther squealed and danced me around the room. "You're my best friend forever!"

When people first go to the Welcome Centre, they usually enter through the back door, checking over their shoulder to see if anyone's watching. Not us. "If people are going to talk, let's give them something to talk about," I said. Esther put on a bright skirt and a polka-dot blouse, and I got into the yellow dress with blue parakeets that Mama got from Mrs. Tafa. We sang all the way as we biked the ten miles to Section Ten and marched in through the Welcome Centre's front door.

A large white bedsheet was draped along the entrance hall. Beside the sheet, a felt marker hung from a string. Dozens of people had used it to write sayings on the sheet: "Everyone is either infected or affected"; "We can't change the past, but we can change the future"; "Where there is love there is life. Where there is life there is hope"; "Live now."

We walked down the hall, past a counseling room, into an open meeting space. In the corner, a group of women, all different ages, and a couple of men, sat around a coffee table next to a piano, having tea and biscuits. Some of them looked healthy; others were very thin. They greeted us with a smile: "Dumêlang."

"Dumêla," Esther said in a loud voice. "I'm here for my appointment."

A large woman got up from the group. She gave Esther a big squeeze. "Dumêla. I'm the counselor, Banyana Kaone."

My jaw dropped. "So this is Banyana Kaone," I thought. "The AIDS Lady in the newspaper who hands out condoms. Up close she doesn't look old and weird. She looks like a mama." Next thing I knew, she was hugging me, too, and suddenly the Welcome Centre felt like home.

Esther and I have been coming every week since. Sometimes more. There's singalongs and card games and potluck suppers. Most of all, there's companionship, the comfort of being with friends who're going through the same thing.

"I'm not alone," says Esther. "I'm alive again."

Mama said I should save my anger to fight injustice. Well, I know what's unjust. The ignorance about AIDS. The shame. The stigma. The silence. The secrets that keep us hiding behind the curtain. The Welcome Centre throws back that curtain. It lets in the fresh air and light.

But it's the only center for miles and miles. No wonder going there seems strange and scary. There need to be centers everywhere.

I think about this as I sit outside, staring at the moon, unable to sleep. I close my eyes and I picture a center in my very own front yard. The Lilian Kabelo Friendship Project.

I burst out laughing. It's a crazy idea. But it's not stupid. I don't need a building. Not right away. I just need a place for people to meet. And I have this yard.

The Lilian Kabelo Friendship Project.

Dreams, dreams, dreams...

ALLAN STRATTON IS AN AWARD-WINNING and internationally published and produced playwright and novelist. In preparation to write *Chanda's Secrets*, Allan traveled to South Africa, Zimbabwe, and Botswana, where various agencies introduced him to those living with and working to fight HIV/AIDS. He was invited into homes, aid and education organizations, and mortuaries in city, village, and cattle post. This book was made possible by the guidance and encouragement of the people he met there, including everyone at the Ghetto Artists in Francistown, who do street theatre on HIV/AIDS testing and prevention; the Tshireletso Shining Stars AIDS Awareness Group, an HIV/AIDS day-care centre; COCEPWA (Coping Centre for People Living with HIV/AIDS); the Light and Courage Centre; PACT (Peer Approach to Counseling by Teens); The Kagisano Women's Shelter Project; and the Coady International Institute. Allan lives in Toronto.